The
Strange
Grave
of
MIKEY
DUNBAR

T0017618

ALSO BY JEREMY JOHN

Robert's Hill (or The Time I Pooped My Snowsuit) and Other Christmas Stories

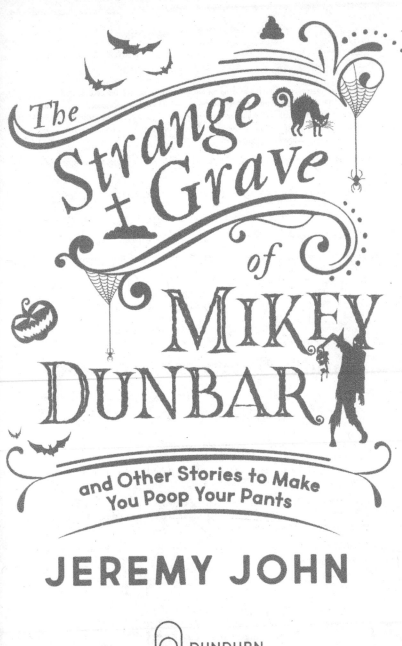

The
Strange
Grave
of
MIKEY
DUNBAR

and Other Stories to Make
You Poop Your Pants

JEREMY JOHN

DUNDURN
PRESS

Publisher: Kwame Scott Fraser | Acquiring editor: Chris Houston
Cover designer: Laura Boyle
Cover image: istock.com/9george; istock.com/difinbeker

Library and Archives Canada Cataloguing in Publication

Title: The strange grave of Mikey Dunbar : and other stories to make you poop your pants / Jeremy John.
Names: John, Jeremy, author.
Identifiers: Canadiana (print) 2022026368X | Canadiana (ebook) 20220263736 | ISBN 9781459751071 (softcover) | ISBN 9781459751088 (PDF) | ISBN 9781459751095 (EPUB)
Classification: LCC PS8619.O4445 S77 2022 | DDC C813/.6—dc23

We acknowledge the support of the Canada Council for the Arts and the Ontario Arts Council for our publishing program. We also acknowledge the financial support of the Government of Ontario, through the Ontario Book Publishing Tax Credit and Ontario Creates, and the Government of Canada.

Printed and bound in Canada.

Dundurn Press
1382 Queen Street East
Toronto, Ontario, Canada M4L 1C9
dundurn.com, @dundurnpress

THESE STORIES ARE DEDICATED TO two specific groups of people who don't normally get along: teachers and students. Their opposing agendas make them natural enemies, but in this case they worked together. Numerous teachers invited me into their classrooms to talk about writing and to share writing exercises. Lots of students participated in those writing exercises, often doing more than the minimum required to get a passing grade. Many of the ideas and topics those students suggested became the stories in this book.

Thank you, teachers, for the honour of being in your classrooms and sharing the joy of engaging with young learners. Thank you, students, for your great ideas and infectious enthusiasm for frightening vampires, disgusting zombies, and gruesome mummies.

If any of those teachers or students are reading this, please remember, this book would not be possible without your contribution, collaboration, and input. Also, by reading this you waive all rights to any royalties.

The author is not responsible for any side effects caused by the reading of this book. These stories may cause TERROR, FEAR, NIGHTMARES, waking HORROR, INSOMNIA, or FATIGUE. Reading *The Strange Grave of Mikey Dunbar and Other Stories to Make You Poop Your Pants* by Jeremy John may induce symptoms that include (but are not limited to) TREMBLING, SHAKING, SHIVERS, or JITTERS. It may even cause extreme cases of the HEEBIE-JEEBIES, the WHIM-WHAMS, or the WILLIES. In rare cases afflictions known as "FRAIDY FINGERS" and "SCAREDY-PANTSNESS" can occur. You have been warned....

CONTENTS

THE HANGMAN

HANGMAN'S HILL WAS JUST OUTSIDE of town. A large grass-covered hill where a lone tree stood in the centre. That is the only marker that signifies it as Hangman's Hill. There is no sign, but everyone in the nearby town knows the name. Hangman's Hill is where you were buried after you were hanged. Since only the worst criminals were sentenced to be hanged, they could not be buried in the church cemetery. Instead, they went to Hangman's Hill. There you would find no crosses or gravestones, just unmarked graves. No person ever visited the hill except for the hangman. At least, no living person.

He was the opposite of what most people expected in a hangman. He was educated, having formal training in math, physics, anatomy, and biology. He may have been the most educated man in town. He was distinguished. He wore store-bought clothes and shining, buckled shoes. He never drank, smoked, or chewed tobacco and always attended church on Sunday. Plus, he was rich.

As the town's hangman, he was on the government's payroll. The hangman received a handsome packet of cash each week from the mayor. So he never had to worry about whether his crops would sell or fear losing his farm if there was a drought.

Also, his unique role meant he paid no taxes and was given a large plot of land when he moved to town. The reasoning being that no one would want to sell land to a hangman and the tax collector would refuse to visit a man who killed people for a living. Plus, since the role of executioner didn't require constant work, he was able to keep several jobs on the side. He worked a small farm that included a few crops, a dozen or so head of cattle, and he even employed a few farmhands to care for his land. Plus, with his education, he often worked as a backup to the town doctor. Many people were uncomfortable with the idea of being treated by the hangman and would avoid going to see him. But others went to him specifically because he was the hangman. Since the hangman lived a quiet life and his house was well outside of town, it made him the perfect doctor when townspeople were afflicted with something embarrassing. If a cowpoke or ranch hand went to the saloon and woke up the next morning with a hangover, a broken nose, or something else that they didn't want people gossiping about, they would choose to see the hangman over the doctor. There was less chance of the news of the medical predicament getting back to their boss or preacher, or worse, their wife. Despite his wealth, education, and good graces, the hangman was shunned by most people in town.

He sat alone each Sunday in church. He ate alone at restaurants. No one ever asked him to attend the dances. Whenever he went into town to do his shopping, he'd quickly find he had the store to himself. He'd walk into the tailor's or the general store and all conversation would stop. Mothers would shoo their children out the door with whispered orders not to stare. Men would make excuses to the shopkeeper about needing to come back later. Inevitably, within seconds of entering the store, the hangman would find he suddenly had the shopkeeper's undivided attention. The hangman would notice the children's stares and the hasty departures with little concern. If anything, it made shopping easier. If he walked into the apothecary to find a line up, it would quickly shrink as each of the people in line in front of him decided they needed to be somewhere else, anywhere else, at that exact moment. That part never bothered him. It was the end of the transactions that made him feel alone. As was the custom, the shopkeepers in town should be sure to shake your hand and ask you to come back before you left the store. But everyone was reluctant to shake the hangman's hand. And it wasn't just shopkeepers. The sheriff, the judge, the mayor, people who knew him very well, even the workers on his own ranch refused to shake his hand. There was the belief that the hangman could measure you for a noose just by shaking your hand. People thought that each time the hangman shook your hand he was judging your height and weight, then remembering that info, in case he ever had to take you out to Hangman's Hill.

In order to do his job properly, the hangman needed to know your exact weight and height. This is why his education was so important to his job. Knowing your height and weight meant that the hangman could then properly perform your execution. All his calculations needed to be exact. If he was to write it out on a chalkboard, it would be the force of the drop minus the mass times the acceleration of gravity on a stationary object. But in practice, all that mattered was that if he did everything right, justice would be served. The proper length of rope, the proper drop speed, with the perfect knot meant that the criminal would fall to the end of the rope and die instantly.

With the correct length of rope, the condemned person would fall to the end of the rope and stop perfectly in place. If the rope length was calculated correctly, the body would be immobilized, hanging perfectly still at the end of the line. No swinging or spinning — in the executioner's world it was called a "hangman's drop."

If the drop speed was correct, the criminal's neck would break and their life would end in an instant. If the body reached the exact right speed at the exact moment that rope ended, there would be a single small but distinct cracking sound from the base of the convict's neck, just above the shoulders.

If the knot was tied correctly, it would tighten in an instant. Staying where it was set, between the sixth and seventh bones in the criminal's neck. If the knot was perfect, it would crush those two neck bones like eggshells.

Doing everything right meant the punishment was quick and painless. If the hangman did his job correctly, then justice would be served. Doing any of these things incorrectly meant torture and cruelty.

If the knot was tied or positioned incorrectly, the noose could slip up to the throat and tighten too late. That would mean that the criminal was not killed quickly. Instead, they may be left to suffocate at the end of the rope. A cruelty that could leave them twitching and gasping for twenty minutes or more.

If the drop speed was wrong for the height and weight of the criminal, they could swing at the end of the rope. Instead of dropping and falling inert at the end of the rope, the body would whip around the gallows, banging into the supports and swinging toward the gathered witnesses. While the effect was still lethal, it was not desired. The hangman wanted the witnesses to leave knowing that justice was done. It was to be solemn and dignified, to have the convicted flopping at the end of the noose was not what he wanted.

If the rope was too long, the convict would fall too far, and the end would be violent and gruesome. If the convicted person fell for just a fraction of a second too long, the hangman risked decapitating the convict. Like the whip of a buggy driver, the snap at the end of the rope could build up enough momentum to pull the criminal's head off. To the horror of those gathered to witness the hanging.

Granted, all hangings had the same result: strangulation or decapitation, the convicted criminal died either way. However, the goal was civilized justice, not a barbaric spectacle. The townsfolk, sheriff, deputies, the judge, and lawyers would be at the hanging to witness the event.

But often there would also be family members of the condemned person there as well. The hangman always believed that those people had suffered as well, not only did they have a criminal in the family, but they also had to endure a public trial. Those folks deserved a solemn administration of justice.

A botched execution could also cause very serious issues for the town. If the state courts heard that a convict was strangled on the gallows, or worse, decapitated, the hangman would be removed. Since there were few people in that line of work, if a town lost its hangman, they were most likely gone forever. No one wanted that. The hangman was a deterrent. His presence kept crimes, serious crimes, to a minimum. For things like fighting or petty theft or being drunk in public, the local sheriff had his ways to deal with those types of criminals. Those people would learn their lesson with a broken nose, a small fine, or a night in the county jail. But when there was a serious crime, the courthouse was opened to the public and the hangman built a gallows where everyone could see it.

The hangman only worked a few times a year, but when he did his work needed to be public and legal. The letter of the law had to be followed in every detail from arrest to trial to execution or absolution. The hangman's work also needed to be public in order to prevent the next crime. The community needed to witness that justice had been done and understand that if they broke the law, the same fate would wait for them.

That is exactly what happened when Martin Breslow was arrested for murder. There was a trial, a conviction, and then a hanging. What was different in this case was the victim. In this case a child had been murdered. The hangman had been called to hang lots of men and even a few women for a number of crimes. Murder, horse theft, and escaping jail were the most common. But the death of a child was a horrendous crime and it had never happened in this town before.

The arrest and trial were quick, Breslow was a drifter who had been working at a farm just on the outskirts of town. Breslow had only been there for a few days when he was found burying the little girl's body. His signed confession made the trial very quick, as did Breslow's refusal to say anything during the trial. After he was sentenced to hang, there was a meeting at the courthouse.

The sheriff, mayor, judge, and of course, the hangman were all in attendance. They met in the judge's office. A cool and quiet place to chat on a hot summer night. Other than those four men, the building was empty, and since the judge's office had no windows, there was no chance of anyone listening in. As the men arrived, within minutes of each other, they sat in silence gathered around a large table across from the judge's desk.

The sheriff was the last to arrive and the first to speak and demanded that the convicted man be killed. "I know the difference between a crook and a killer, and he's neither. A crook just wants to take something, and if someone has to die for him to get it, then oh well." The sheriff was seated at the long table in the middle of the judge's chambers, cowboy hat on his lap. "A killer is smart," he continued. "Usually is getting well paid to do the job, but he has no desire to go to jail and will head out of town as soon as he can. But this is different. This drifter had no reason to do what he did. The faster we send his soul to hell the better." When the sheriff was done, he crossed himself and stared down at his boots.

The judge spoke next. "This man has been tried and convicted, but I don't know if he should be executed. He never even spoke once. Not to you, sheriff, not to his lawyer, and not once while he was on trial. We know that he understands, he signed the confession. He nods or shakes his head when you ask him simple questions. But I'm not sure he realizes that he's going to be executed. He might be some kind of simpleton?"

The sheriff was quick to answer yes. Clear and emphatic, he said, "Simple or not, he killed that little girl. He's got to hang."

The mayor got out of his seat and moved to stand at the corner of the table. He was a fair and honest politician and he knew how to command attention. By standing, he knew he would give the impression of strength and authority. Walking to the corner of the table allowed him to be seen and heard by everyone. "This town is a powder keg; those citizens are angry and they want justice. The sheriff is right. The sooner that man is swinging from a rope the better."

The judge got up from behind his desk and poured a glass of water from a tall pitcher on his desk. He brought it over to the sheriff, a man who he'd worked with for many years and had been friends with for even longer, and said, "All he ever did was nod or shake his head. The only reason we know he can speak is 'cause he told the rancher his name when he was hired. There is clearly something not right in his head. He may be a simpleton, he may be something else. But we can't send a man like that to the gallows." He slid the glass of water to the sheriff and watched as the sheriff took a drink. The judge was giving his friend the silence he needed to think about the heavy questions in his mind before he spoke again. "There is a proper prison in the next county. Let's ship him there. Let him be their problem. He can rot in a cell, and God can decide when he dies."

Since everyone else in the room had made their feelings clear, they all turned to the one who had yet to cast their vote. The hangman was busy reading the sheriff's report. He made a note in the margin of the autopsy report the town doctor had written. Then he turned the page over and scratched down a short calculation before looking up at the men who were waiting for him to speak.

Not used to making speeches or even talking too much at all, he took his time thinking about what he should say. "This isn't a question of who should decide his fate. This is a question of did you all do your jobs right. The way I see it, you did." As he spoke he looked directly at each of the men in the room.

"Sheriff, you arrested this man. You apprehended him without prejudice and held him for trial without malice or ill intent. This report and the doctor's examination of the deceased were clear and thorough." He nodded at the sheriff and the sheriff nodded back.

"Your Honour," he said with a nod to the judge. "The trial was fair with both the prosecution and the defence given an equal say, as it were. Your assessment of the accused, for what it is, is accurate and valuable."

"Mr. Mayor, the law is clear." He said looking up at the politician. The mayor may have still been standing at the corner of the table, but the hangman was the one controlling the room. "He was fairly arrested and tried; he's guilty, justice needs to be done. You all did your jobs correctly. Now I will do mine."

With that, the meeting was over. The hangman said goodbye but left without offering to shake anyone's hand. He knew it made people uncomfortable, so he avoided it when possible. He headed home and began his plans for the hanging.

Building the gallows would take a few days, and as always, they would be built beside the jailhouse. Putting the platform along the west wall of the building would ensure the afternoon sun on the day of the hanging. Plus, there was a large space between the jailhouse and the bank next door. That would allow enough room for the townsfolk to gather as witnesses.

The hangman had plenty of work to do. He would need to level the ground, pick up the lumber, construct the gallows, and then test his equipment. But before he would begin any of that, he made a trip to the jail. The hangman measured and weighed the convicted man as he always had done in the past. Then he did something he had never done before. He asked the sheriff if he could sit and speak with Martin Breslow.

The sheriff agreed as long as the cell stayed locked and the hangman kept his distance. The sheriff knew that the hangman was very smart, too smart to let his guard down around a prisoner, but he brought the hangman a chair anyway. "Make sure you keep yourself seated," the sheriff said as he placed a high-backed wooden chair in front of the cell doors, sliding it into place about four feet from the bars. The hangman understood. He sat firmly in the chair and nodded at the sheriff. Both men knew that people who were headed to be hanged could get desperate. Even the quiet ones. If the hangman got too close to the bars — maybe let his guard down during the conversation — the criminal was likely to reach out from his cell and grab the hangman. Then the sheriff would have a hostage situation, where the hostage-taker had nothing to lose.

The sheriff looked from the prisoner to the hangman and back again. He knew what the hangman wanted: answers. There were too many questions without answers. The sheriff had been doing his job for long enough to know that the answers were never satisfactory. There was no good answer for "Why did you do it?" But in every case, over all those years, he had always heard an answer. But not this time. The sheriff left the hangman to ask his questions and hoped he would get one of those unsatisfactory answers.

The hangman looked the prisoner over. He was small in every way. Short and skinny, almost scrawny. The hangman looked at the prisoner's hands, folded neatly on his lap. They were tiny, too. Made the hangman think that the prisoner probably made for a lousy worker. He had hired a few workers in his time and he'd learned that small workers are slow workers. Mucking out the stables, feeding the pigs, herding the cattle. Every job was harder for the smaller workers. That's probably why this little man couldn't find steady work. He'd get hired by a rancher who was short on workers and when someone stronger and faster would come along, the little guy would be out of a job and off to the next town to look for another rancher that was in a pinch.

That, or he'd drift out of town to keep from getting caught. Maybe he'd find work somewhere, spend a week or so blending in, looking for his next victim. Then he'd strike and move on to the next town to do it all again. Maybe he had been doing it for years. There could be a string of dead little girls right across the state. Just this time he got caught before he could drift to another town.

Either way, he looked unlike any farmhand the hangman had ever seen.

After twenty minutes or so, the hangman left his chair outside the cell and walked to the sheriff's office at the front of the building. He knew what the sheriff was going to say, so before he could ask the question, the hangman answered it. "Nothing," he stated before he was even all the way in the room. "Never even said a single word." The sheriff nodded, he was hoping there would have been something but he never expected it. "Can I ask what you plan on serving the prisoner for dinner tonight?" the hangman inquired. The question caught the sheriff off guard, no one had ever asked what a criminal was going to eat. "Ah …my wife usually makes soup and bread for the boys, I was just going to give him some of that." The hangman nodded and asked if he could bring the prisoner dinner that night. The sheriff agreed, thinking maybe a small kindness like a home-cooked meal might get the prisoner to talk.

The hangman worked on the gallows for the rest of the day. He stopped only to send one of his farmhands to the lumber mill to place his order. When the worker returned, he was dispatched to fetch food for the prisoner. When the meal arrived, and the hangman was done grading and levelling the ground beside the jailhouse, he headed inside once again.

The sheriff and his men were just about to enjoy their soup and fresh loaves when the hangman walked in. He presented the meal to the sheriff. Carefully, the sheriff emptied the basket of food out on his desk. He then transferred each item into the shallow tin pans that the prisoners ate from. The pans were light and made of tin, no sharp edges or hard corners. There was no way they could be used as weapons or tools to escape. There was no cutlery, of course, the prisoners ate everything with their hands or drank out of the shallow pans directly. The approved containers were also specifically sized, just large enough to fit under the gap at the bottom of the cell door. Moving the food into the prison dishes also allowed the sheriff to check the food. Not that he suspected the hangman would try to poison the convict or that he would try to hide something in the food to help him escape. But investigating the food was jailhouse policy.

For dinner the two men sat in the back of the building. One on his chair, placed again by the sheriff a safe distance from the bars of the cell. The other man sitting on the floor eating with his fingers. He popped cubed pieces of beef in his mouth, then sucked on the sauce that covered his fingers. It was rich and thick; the hangman described it using a few French words that meant nothing to the man in the cell. All he knew was that it tasted of cream and butter. After he had eaten all the beef, he moved to the slices of roasted potatoes. Again, he savoured the creamy sauce and herbs that covered the dish. Even tearing pieces off the fresh loaf of bread he was given and dipping them in the sauce. Dessert was a small sugar pie. A thick but flaky crust filled with a mixture of brown sugar, cream, and butter. The prisoner ate everything while the hangman asked him questions. Although he seemed to be listening, he never once said a single word.

And that was the routine that the hangman quickly fell into. Breakfast outside the prisoner's cell. The hangman asked questions while the prisoner ate flapjacks with honey. Then he'd head outside to continue building the gallows. He'd break for lunch and head back to his wooden chair in the jailhouse. The hangman would ask the prisoner questions while he ate in silence. Chicken with grits and gravy, or maybe cornbread and beef stew. A slice of apple pie with a chunk of cheddar cheese for dessert. Then back to work on the gallows until dinner back at the jailhouse. Flank steak with baked potatoes and a slice of pecan pie at the end. The hangman even started bringing candies that he picked up at the general store to try and loosen the man's tongue. But he never said a word.

Each meal was the same. The sheriff would take apart each dish and inspect it as he put it in the prison-approved dishes. The hangman would slide them carefully under the bars of the cell door. Then the prisoner would finish every bite, often using the bread or rolls to soak up the rich sauces after the meat or fish was gone. Then he'd slide the empty pans back under the cell door without ever saying a word to his generous host.

By the time the prisoner had eaten his sixth supper, the gallows were finished. As the hangman collected his dishes, the sheriff came out of his office. The look on the hangman's face told the sheriff the answer to his question without even needing to ask. The hangman answered it anyway, "Not even so much as a thank you."

It was then that one of the three deputies spoke out, saying something they had all been thinking but hadn't dared to say out loud. "The damned killer eats better than me and my kids." The deputy was the youngest and newest hire in the group. Standing beside the jailhouse door, arms crossed, he spoke toward the floor. The sheriff quickly stood up and was starting to cross the floor. He was on his way to loudly remind the inexperienced deputy about his place in the town's legal system and the respect he needed to show his superiors. But the hangman moved first. He stepped in front of the sheriff, cutting him off from the deputy, who was about to be very sorry he said those words out loud.

The hangman stepped up in front of the deputy, looking down into the eyes of the slightly shorter man. "Why deputy," he said, then quickly closed the gap between the two men. The hangman and the deputy were toe to toe. The hangman's eyes were running up and down the deputy, scanning from his head to his toes and back again, while the deputy looked from the floor to the other deputies to the face of his angry boss. The hangman ran his eyes once more to the top of the deputy's head and squinted like he was trying to remember something. Then grabbed the scared man's right hand in his, shaking it firmly and looking him dead straight in the eyes, saying, "I'd be happy to host you and your family for a meal on any day of your choosing." The hangman pumped the deputy's hand once toward the floor before letting go and heading for home.

The next day was the hanging.

Scheduled for four o'clock.

It would be over in minutes.

The prisoner would not eat that day. The hangman knew it was best not to feed the convict the day of the hanging. A full stomach could make for a messy ordeal.

The local priest came to the jailhouse at about three thirty and offered to hear Breslow's confession. He never said a word. Every step from the jail cell outside to the gallows, Breslow never said a word.

The crowd outside the jailhouse was huge. It looked to the hangman that most of the town had come to see the execution, which was just what he wanted. He was a deterrent. He wanted everyone around to know that the law, and the gallows, could be waiting for them.

The crowd booed and screamed at the convicted man as he was led out the front door of the jailhouse. Again, exactly what the hangman wanted. The townsfolk were angry, and they had every right to be angry. Screaming at the convicted man helped them let some of their anger out. Another reason why the executions were public. Folks needed a release, and in a few moments, when they heard the small short crack, they would all feel much better.

The hangman met Breslow, the sheriff, and his deputies at the bottom of the stairs leading up to the platform that the hangman had built. He nodded to the sheriff to signify that he had the prisoner and slid a black felt bag over the prisoner's head.

The bag was there for a few key reasons. First, to shield the witnesses from one of the more gruesome effects of a hanging. Quite often, even if the hangman did everything perfectly, the prisoner's eyes would burst. A side effect of the rapid pressure to the head, it was best that the people gathered never saw that.

More importantly, it helped keep the prisoner calm. The last few steps to the noose were where the convict was most likely to panic. If they were going to scream or cry or fight, this was where it was going to happen. Again, not what the hangman wanted the witnesses to see. He wanted them to see a criminal who had done wrong, been caught, and accepted their punishment as just.

The hangman led Breslow, arms tied and head covered, up the nine stairs from the ground to the platform with the trap door in the middle. As the hangman moved the prisoner into the middle of the trap door, the mayor walked · to the edge of the platform closest to the crowd and began his speech.

It was short and solemn. The mayor talked about bringing justice and restoring peace while the hangman looped the noose around the prisoner's neck. Walking through his calculations in his mind, knowing that each one had been checked and re-checked before the first nail was struck, he tightened the noose. The knot was tight and high on the convict's neck. The knot sat just below his right ear, pointing straight out from the side of his neck before the rope went up to the crossbar directly above where the man stood. Everything was just as the hangman had planned. The perfect knot, the perfect speed, the perfect length of rope. All he needed was the signal. When the mayor was done speaking, he nodded to the judge. It was his turn to perform his duty, and record any final words. Of course, there were none. After a silence, the judge nodded to the hangman.

That was the signal.

The lever was pulled, the trap door opened, and Breslow fell.

The perfect knot, the perfect speed, the perfect length of rope.

There was a gasp from the crowd and a loud, repeating snap from the man's neck. Loud enough to echo off the wall of the bank across the lane. When the sound left the spot under the platform and rebounded back to the hangman's ears, he knew everything had worked according to his plan.

After the lever is pulled, there are a number of activities that all need to happen quickly. The sheriff and his deputies start politely dispersing the crowd. The hangman unties the body and places it in a coffin waiting nearby. The city buys the wooden coffin, it is made from rough wood and has as few nails as possible. The coffin is loaded into a small wagon and begins the journey to Hangman's Hill.

The gallows will remain in place for a few days. Through the weekend townsfolk will get quiet as they pass it. Parents will point it out to kids and remind them to behave themselves. Drunks headed out from the saloon will take the long way home to avoid the street where it sits. But the wood is precious and it is soon reclaimed by the hangman to use on his farm. Same with the rope. Good rope is rare and expensive. The hangman will avoid ever cutting it, if at all possible.

When the two travellers got to their destination, one just visiting, one to stay forever, the coffin was unloaded and the body placed in a shallow grave on the side of the hill facing away from town. The hangman lifted the convict out of the rough coffin and dropped him in the hole. Nothing gentle, no ceremony or solemn sense of occasion. The body was just pushed and pulled until all the limbs were in the hole. The hangman untied his wrists, removed the hood, and knelt down in the grass beside the grave.

Looking down into the convict's eyes, the hangman said, "I know you can hear me."

The hangman leaned in a little farther, staring at the eyes of the man in the grave. He watched for a twitch or a blink, maybe a change in the pupil. But he saw nothing.

"Everything was correct," he said. "The perfect knot, the perfect speed, the perfect length of rope."

The hangman continued to stare, hoping for some sign of understanding.

"In the medical books, it's called a 'pseudo-coma,'" the hangman said. Then he held his hand out over the criminal's face, shielding the man's eyes from the sun. The hangman watched as the criminal's pupils dilated, just as his medical training had taught him they would. The hangman watched as the dark circles in the centres of the criminal's eyes slowly grew larger in the shade. Then the hangman pulled his hand back and watched the criminal's pupils shrink as the sunlight hit his eyes. He was unable to blink, but the hangman knew that the killer was still in there.

"I prefer the layman's term, 'locked-in syndrome,'" he said, picking up where he had left off. "It describes what has happened to you so well. You are locked in there, and you will never get out."

The hangman smiled, not in arrogance but in satisfaction for a job well done. He had set himself a difficult task and he had succeeded.

"The weight was tricky," he admitted. "A little wisp of a thing like you would never be able to generate the kind of force needed to break those bones at the top of your neck. Sure, breaking the usual ones would have been no trouble, but that wouldn't have been right. You needed to be a whole lot heavier if things were going to be done right, and it looks like I've done things right. Total body paralysis, but you can still hear, you can still think, and you can still feel."

With that, the hangman pulled a short sharp knife out of his pocket and stuck it in the convict's chest. He placed the blade perfectly, right into the man's pectoral muscle on the right side of his chest. He was too well trained to cut too deep. He stabbed just deep enough to cut through the muscle and hit the very sensitive nerve endings that surround the rib cage. Then the hangman saw what he was waiting for: tears. An involuntary response to pain, and proof that his plan had worked. Breslow's neck was broken in just the right place. Where he would be totally defenceless but still able to feel pain.

The hangman leaned back, withdrawing and pocketing his knife. "It was the weight that bothered me." And then he said, "Again, not for a proper hanging. You were plenty heavy for that, but if I was going to do what I did, I needed to add a few pounds to your frame. I'm glad you liked eating so much. If you hadn't eaten all that rich food and those buttery sauces and sweet desserts, I'm not sure what I would have done. I mean, I could have added rocks in your pockets or maybe weights on your shoes, but that would have been very suspicious. And I sure couldn't have the sheriff or the judge or the mayor getting wind of what I planned to do with you. They would never understand. Not like I do."

The hangman looked over the body that was stretched out in the shallow grave in front of him. Hands crossed on his chest, legs tucked tight together, Breslow could have passed for any other dead body that the hangman had seen during his lifetime. If it wasn't for the eyes. Normally, the eyes of the corpse are peacefully closed, these were wide open and terrified. The killer wasn't really sure what had happened, or why. But he knew that whatever the hangman was going to do to him, he was unable to stop him and he would have to watch while it happened.

"They would never understand," the hangman repeated, looking into the killer's eyes. Hoping to see some understanding behind the fear. "It's all thanks to my education. As you may now realize, my education gives me a special insight when it comes to things like force, momentum, the human body, and death. See, when I looked at the doctor's report, what you did to that little girl, a man your size, there would be no way a man that small could inflict those kinds of wounds. A man that size, to hurt a kid like that, he'd have to be enraged. That attack was savage, vicious. That doctor's report wasn't about a murder, it was about an attack by a wild animal. Those other lawmen don't have the education to understand what you did to that little girl. The sheriff said you were either a crook or a killer, but you're neither. You're a monster. Yes, you should die, but you don't deserve to die like a human."

The hangman looked south, back toward the town, over the crest of Hangman's Hill. Tears poured down the sides of Breslow's head as he lay immobilized in the shallow grave. He still did not know what was going to happen to him, but he knew it was going to be worse than dying and it had been planned by a man who knew everything about the human body, about pain, about death.

The hangman continued, still staring out at the town. "Those other men said we should leave your fate to God, or decide your fate for ourselves. But they don't understand. They read the doctor's report, but they will never really understand what you did. So what else was I to do? If we decided your fate, it would be too quick. If we left it up to God, we'd never know if justice was done."

The hangman stood up quickly, brushed the dirt and bits of grass off his knees, then looked down at the convicted man one last time.

"That's why I'm leaving you here. Like this," he said. "Maybe what will happen is that some bugs might find you and eat your eyes. Or maybe it will be crows that come first to tear off your lips and your cheeks. Maybe you're going to watch as a hungry coyote approaches. You're going to see it coming. You're going to feel its teeth. And there is nothing you can do to stop it."

With that, the hangman left. Tears streamed down the sides of the convict's head. He'd been hanged, as justice demanded, but the hangman had delivered vengeance as well.

DADDY-DAUGHTER HALLOWEEN

HE CURLED HIS CAPE AROUND his thin torso, with only his piercing eyes peering over the black satin. Looking down at his young apprentice, he instructed her on the night ahead. "When the sky is dark and the moon is full, we will strike," he said. "We will gorge ourselves, moving from house to house, taking all that we want, not stopping until we have had our fill."

"Oh, come on, Dad," said the young girl at his side. "You're embarrassing me."

Her father turned to her, stern and cold. "This is our way," he growled. "Since the dawn of time our people have hunted on this night, and so shall we hunt."

She had seen this before; he was going to make a speech to her. He always seemed to be doing that. She doubted that he had been practising in the mirror, but she had no doubt he had been thinking about making this speech for a very long time. Interrupting would only make the speech longer, her only option was to roll her eyes and let him finish.

"For centuries we have owned the night. Spreading terror wherever we choose." He was pointing out into the darkness, she knew he was trying to be dramatic. It might have worked, too, if his outfit wasn't so ridiculous. "Our kind has hunted in all the lands of this earth. Known as *chupacabra* to some, *bantu* to others. We are called *baka* on some islands and *kasha* on others. In ancient Rome, we were named *nosferatu* and today, vampires."

"Not the history lesson again," she whispered as she rolled her eyes. She was quiet and it was very dark, but she knew that he heard and saw her. He ignored her and continued with the same speech she had heard every Halloween night before they went out.

"But whatever their terrified minds call us, this has always remained the same: On this night, we hunt!" He threw his cape to the side in a flourish and stuck out his chest to display his elegantly tailored black vest and white shirt. It had been a year since she had seen him in these clothes; she wondered if he was ever going to get a new outfit.

She stared at the large white ruffles at the collar surrounding his neck and the lace sleeves that hung out of the dark grey coat almost completely covering his hands. He was wearing numerous large, gaudy rings on each hand. She wondered how he was going to be able to carry anything tonight, she was starting to think that she was going to have to do everything herself.

"Oh, you are so old," she said. He pretended not to hear her.

"This night," he continued, "All Hallows Eve, when the thin veil between the.living and the dead is torn asunder and we are released once again to feed on the citizens of this world." He laughed, closing his eyes and throwing his head back.

"Stop, Dad," she said. "Someone is going to see us." She pulled him by his elbow off of the stone steps they were standing on and into the shadow of the nearby tree. Their home was far from the rest of the town. It was a dark and moonless night, so very little chance that anyone would see them. Still, she didn't want to risk being seen with her dad, especially not dressed like this.

"We are vampires, this is what we do," he bellowed.

"Yeah, I know," she pleaded. "But do we have to? Like, do we *have* to?"

He was trying to follow what she was saying, but as she often did, she had lost him. "I don't know what you mean," he admitted.

"Like this outfit, it's nice but —" she started.

"You don't like it?" he interrupted. "I picked it out just for you. It's very modern, I thought you'd like it."

"Oh, it's very lovely, thank you," she began, "but not practical is it? Like this corset."

"Real whalebone," her father interjected.

"Yes, it's lovely," she repeated. "But it makes it really hard to move around, it's so tight. And this dress is so long." She stood on one leg and stuck her foot out in front of her to show that he could barely see the end of her pointed shoe sticking out from under the lace at the hem. "And the gloves?" she held her hands out for her father to see. "Are the gloves necessary? I mean, if we get busy, I'm going to want my hands free, and it's not like I'm going to get cold tonight."

"But it's tradition. We do this every year," he said. It was clear that she had hurt his feelings. "If we don't dress like this, then how will they know we are vampires?"

"I know, Dad," she said, hoping that he would understand but knowing that he wouldn't. "But just 'cause that's how we've dressed in the past, does that mean we have to do it that way? Like, forever?"

He decided to put his foot down. "Yes, this is how it is done. Tradition is important. There have been too many changes around here already." He pointed to the cellphone in her hand. "You're lucky I even let you bring that thing along."

She didn't know what to say, this night was important to him, more than any other night. It was a special night and it was always their night out together. She decided not to argue and risk upsetting him further.

"Now, let's go," he said. His tone was softer now, he was trying after all, and she knew how much he liked this night. Going out. Getting all dressed up. Filling their bellies all night long and then laughing about it all when they got back home just before sunrise. "But please put that thing away, just for tonight," he said as he glanced down at the phone still in her hand.

"Sure, Dad, let's head out. Just you and me." She smiled up at him and they were about to step out into the cool night air when she said, "But what if there was a boy?"

Her father froze in his tracks, his eyes staring off into the night. Looking out past the gnarled trees that surrounded their property. In the village down the road, he could clearly see the boys and girls moving from house to house.

She was in too deep now to take it back and repeated herself. "What if there was a boy, and he was expecting to meet me tonight?"

"What boy?" her father asked coldly, not turning his gaze from the village directly ahead in the distance. Staring off into the distance, he could see the small cottage with the crooked chimney. When he used his supernatural senses he could hear the children. Their voices, their footsteps, the echoes of "trick-or-treat" rolling up from the village, making him hungry, making him wish he was down there with the children.

"This boy," she said brightly as she unlocked her phone to show him a picture. "His name is Trevor. He's expecting to meet me tonight ... in about thirty minutes." And then she swiped to the right to reveal another picture of a smiling boy. "I'm supposed to meet him in an hour, his name is Carl. Then there's this guy," another swipe, a different smiling boy, "I'm supposed to meet him at nine. I think he said his name is D.J."

Her father was incensed, standing as still as a marble statue, but she knew that inside he was furious and about to explode. "Please, let me explain." She needed to be quick. "I didn't use my real name and the picture, of course, isn't me." She saw her father's shoulders relax just a little bit, or maybe she imagined it. Either way, she continued with her plan. "See, they've each agreed to meet me tonight. A secluded place in the forest, where there are no lights, no cameras, lots of shadows, lots of hiding places. I staggered the meetings so that there are thirty minutes in between each one. We'll have plenty of time to eat, dispose of the body, and hide before the next boy arrives."

"Have you learned nothing?" he hissed in her face. "Never the young, feeding on the young only invites issues."

"Yes, Dad, I know." She had been holding this in for a long time, it felt good to finally say the words out loud. "But things have changed, and we can, too. I understand that there was a time when only taking drifters or vagabonds made sense." Her father was about to tell her why when she interrupted, making his points for him. "They are less likely to have families, fewer people who are concerned about them when they go missing, and the authorities will spend less time looking for them. That all makes sense, but with a little bit of planning, maybe doing things a little bit differently, we could have a feast."

She felt a little like she was cheating, appealing to his hunger when it had been an entire year since he had eaten, but she was hungry, too. And she really did have a better plan.

"How long has it been since you hunted something young?" she cooed. "Two, maybe three hundred years? Think about it: sweet, rich, thick blood. Pulsing through a strong young neck. The excitement of taking a life in its prime. The feeling of power when they try to push you away, the look in their eyes when their hands hit your chest and they feel your strength as you pull them in. You are an unstoppable hunter and they are powerless prey, and just before you drink their blood, you get to see that realization in their eyes. And that look is almost as good as the taste of their blood."

She might have overdone it. He wasn't saying anything.

"Am I wrong?" she asked.

Silence.

"Are you not the world's greatest hunter? Are you not the perfect killing machine? Made to spread terror in the hearts of any human who hears your name?"

Silence.

She leaned in, closer to him. As if she could only whisper what she was about to say. Afraid to have anyone else overhear. "Or are you a leech? Cursed to rise once a year to sip the thin pale blood of this world's forgotten and abandoned?"

His response was measured, controlled. He had not survived this long by being reckless. "What happens after this feast of yours? What happens when their parents report them missing? When the police check their phones? When they dig up the entire forest to find the bodies of these missing boys?"

"I will take care of all those things," she assured him. "See, when a boy arrives, I'll ask him to take a picture of us on our first date. He'll think it's cute. When he unlocks his phone, you attack. You move in, you grab his arms, you see the look of terror in the prey's eyes, and you get to feed first." He liked everything about that part of her plan. Before he could object, she continued. "While you do that, I use his phone to update his status. Something about meeting the love of his life. How he is going to move far away and is never coming back. His parents, the police, everyone will be looking for a runaway kid who is far away. They will be looking everywhere else but where we've hidden the bodies. Right here in the town graveyard."

"NO!" he thundered. He was enraged. "We don't kill where —"

"Yes, we don't kill where we sleep," she said, rolling her eyes. "I know, I know. But we'd hide the bodies in the mausoleum. Think about it. There are twelve vaults in there, each with one body. If we hid the bodies in there, no one would ever suspect it. The police could walk right to the mausoleum doors and never think to wonder if there are too many bodies inside. Even if they brought in dogs trained to find corpses, all they would smell is the old rotting bodies. It's the perfect hiding place."

Silence.

Then he smiled.

Her father was actually smiling.

He turned to look at her, then down at her phone, then back to her. "Trevor, you say? Well, let's not keep Trevor waiting."

With that, he grabbed her hand and together they stepped out into the moonlight, away from the stone mausoleum where they slept each day. In a puff of smoke, they turned into bats, one large and one small, and headed off into the Halloween night to hunt something young.

THE STRANGE GRAVE OF
MIKEY DUNBAR, NUMBER I

THERE IS A STRANGE GRAVE far north of here. It sits beneath an old tree, beside an even older pub. The pub is a low stone building with a steep roof and a crumbling chimney that sits at an impossible angle.

It is well off the beaten path, you're unlikely to ever come across it. It was built when a coal mine was opened nearby, and it remains there even though the mine was closed long ago.

The grave is almost blank, except for a few words. There is no cross, no name. Just the four words *buy me a drink* carved into a huge shiny slab of black stone. It is a tombstone, lying flat on the ground. Not a gravestone, standing straight up. This rare piece of stone would have been very heavy, extremely expensive, and only ever used for someone of great importance.

Maybe the strangest thing about this grave is the tradition that surrounds it. Each and every customer at the pub takes the last sip of each drink and pours it on the grave.

If you're ever there on a Wednesday evening or a Sunday afternoon, after the bingo crowd has left the church hall, you will find Hazel there. She is very old, but she's one of those ladies that it's hard to know just how old she really is. She's very small and moves very slowly, but she still manages to live alone and seems to still have all her marbles. She will sit alone at the pub, she has outlived all of her friends and every member of her family. She will sit in one of the more comfortable chairs in the corner of the pub nearest to the fireplace. She will have two Pimm's and then go home before it gets late. The bar only stocks Pimm's for her, it is an old, English summer drink and no one has ever ordered it but her. Most times she sits in silence but if you ask, she will be happy to reminisce about the man buried outside the pub. A musician named Mikey Dunbar.

Before "the big one," which is how she refers to the First World War, there was a local musician who would sing each night at that very pub. He could play any instrument and sang with the voice of an angel. And even though he could play any song after hearing it only once, the song that he got the most requests for was one of his own. It was a beautiful singalong song, perfect for a small pub crowd, called "Buy Me a Drink." While Hazel can still hum the tune, she only remembers the opening verse of the song:

Buy me a drink, said the man to his mates.
Oh, buy me a drink, said the lass to her man.
For tonight I am happy and the stars are
    shining,
But this night will end and 'morrow must dawn.
So buy me a drink, o'er the good times start
    fading.
Please buy me a drink, and we'll hold back
    the sun.

The talented young man would often sing it multiple times a night. Each time it would inspire the bar patrons to buy another round. Men would sing along then order a round for their best mates, or their wives or girlfriends, and very often a drink for the singer himself. It was very good for business.

Before long news of the talented musician spread and he was invited to travel to other towns that had their own pubs and sing there, but he always refused. He would say, "I have everything I need right here. Why would I ever want to leave?" This, of course, was great news to the pub owner, and instead of his greatest attraction heading to other venues, people from all over started to travel to the tiny pub to hear Mikey Dunbar and his song.

For a long time business was very good and the pub owner built a stage and even bought a brand new piano that was shipped all the way from France. Mikey and his song "Buy Me a Drink" became very famous. There were times when the little pub was so full that people would stand in the open doorway of the pub to listen to the young singer. Eventually, the pub owner even started charging people to stand outside the pub's open windows and listen to Mikey play.

Things were very good for the town, the pub, and the singer. Then the war started. Mikey was drafted and died somewhere in Belgium.

His body was shipped back to his family but he was not buried immediately. The town was trying to come up with a special way to honour its favourite son. There was talk of a plaque or adding him to the mausoleum with the town founders. But before a decision could be made, both of Mikey's parents passed away. No doubt of a broken heart after losing their own only child.

It was the pub owner who came up with the idea of a special grave. One that reflected Mikey's impact on the town and how much he was loved. They would build a special tombstone, a huge one that not only had his name and the dates of his birth and death, but also the lyrics to the song that made him, and the only pub he ever played at, so very famous.

The church objected to the glorification of a pub singer and his song about drinking, and refused to let the man be laid to rest in the church graveyard. So it was decided to bury him beside the pub. The tombstone would have to be huge to have the entire song engraved, so after the war a special slab of smooth, black granite was ordered from Italy. By the time it arrived in town, the pub's fortunes had changed and money was very tight. While work had been started on the epitaph, the pub owner refused to pay to have the engraving finished. Therefore the young man was laid to rest with just the first four words of the famous song on his tombstone.

The night that Mikey Dunbar was finally laid to rest. There was no service. No prayers. No party. The pub was closed for the night. The owner didn't want to face the scorn of the patrons who thought — who knew — that Mikey deserved better.

The next day when the pub's regulars arrived, they found the owner drunk and raving about nightmares. He said that every time he fell asleep, he dreamed of Mikey Dunbar. Mikey was chasing him, screaming at the pub owner over and over again "buy me a drink." In the dream, the pub owner stumbles backwards in a muddy army trench while bullets tear Mikey Dunbar to shreds. First his chest is ripped open and then his hand is shot off. Red-hot streaks tear the skin off his face and the dreaming man watches as Mikey's eyes fall into the mud. Fire flashes in front of him and the explosion rips both of his arms away. But all the singer ever does is scream "buy me a drink." He never slows down, he never looks away. With each blast and bullet, Mikey Dunbar continues his relentless chase. Eventually, the dreaming man falls on his back in the mud and is caught. Mikey, in his khaki army uniform, covered in burns and blood, stands over his prey and screams one last time, "Buy me a drink."

Then he falls.

The pub owner is paralyzed in the dream. Unable to move or even scream. He is frozen in place as the thing that used to be his friend falls on top of him. As Mikey drops, the dreamer knows he is about to be pinned to the ground. Trapped between the cold brown mud of the trench and the warm red gore that is pouring from the bullet holes. He cannot move, he cannot look away. As the faceless man lands on top of him, they are both driven down into the mud. The last light from the battlefield disappears and mud seals the grave above them. They are entombed together, one living, one dead, forever.

Then the dream starts over again.

When the pub owner was done telling his customers about his nightmares, they sat in silence until one of the regulars asked, "Is it too late to buy him a drink?" The pub owner grabbed a bottle of whiskey, charged outside, and poured the whole thing onto the grave of Mikey Dunbar. That night the pub owner slept peacefully and he would then declare that everyone should pour out their last sip to avoid having Mikey's ghost visit them that night.

Hazel will say that she has never forgotten to pour out the last sip of her drink. Never. She will then say, "'Tis better to give a sip to the ghost than to end up as one."

She will tell her tale and then pour the last sip of her drink onto the strange grave, knowing that every word of the tale is true.

THE YOUNG KNIGHT AND THE QUEST TO KILL THE WOLDGER

THERE ONCE WAS A BRAVE young knight. Having been given a quest by the king, he headed off into the wilderness. He rode for many days, and although his path was slow and treacherous, he never once doubted his own bravery. After a time just as the sun was about to set, he came to a large stream and he decided that before he stopped for the night he would get a drink for himself and his horse. He climbed down from his tall steed, removed his shining silver helmet, and led the horse to the water's edge.

The stream was very wide and very deep, and with the quickly setting sun it was impossible for him to see the bottom. He scanned the area around him knowing that when he knelt down to drink from the stream, he would be vulnerable to attack. He turned around slowly, staring deeply at every bush and each quickly growing shadow. He saw nothing. He continued to stand in silence at the water's edge, listening for any sign of danger but he heard nothing. Assured of his safety he turned to the stream and knelt down to drink, then he heard a voice say, "I wouldn't do that if I were you."

The brave young knight spun on his heel and drew his sword in a flash. As he turned, he readied himself for a fight. Years of training and a lifetime of practice meant he assumed the proper stance without even thinking. Swinging his right hand around, he pulled his short sword from the scabbard on his hip as he anchored his left foot behind him. Knowing his helmet was on the bank beside him and that he was vulnerable, he immediately raised his left arm up beside his face. His training had taught him that an enemy would try to strike where he is most vulnerable, so he steadied his left arm, bracing for the blow, and hoped that the steel bracer that covered his arm from wrist to elbow would absorb the attack. But none came.

Quickly adjusting from defence to attack, the brave young knight changed his stance. He brought his left leg forward and shifted his weight onto his back foot. He pulled his shining sword to his right hip, being sure to point the blade straight out from the middle of his body. The armour master of the king had taught him that this way, he was ready for any attack, high or low. His left arm was thrust out to his side, ready as the perfect counter-balance for any attack he would need to perform.

He stood ready. The perfect example of his training. Poised and positioned to deal with any enemy. His hand tightened its grip on the handle of his sword while his eyes darted around the area in front of him, looking for his attacker. Then he heard, "I'm sorry."

With that, an old man stepped out from behind a cluster of trees into the clearing by the stream. "I did not mean to startle you so, good sir knight," he said. "But I saw from a distance that you were about to drink from that stream, and it is poisoned."

The knight was not really listening, he had been taught to assess his enemy and the young knight's mind was busy judging the possible danger before him. The man was old and obviously poor. Dressed in rough rags and leathers, he had on dirty boots and carried a large bundle of firewood. The old man was standing perfectly still, with his right arm raised in the air; it was his only arm.

The poor man's left arm was gone. The young knight could see that the sleeve of the man's tunic was tied in a knot. In the loop of his belt was a short but sturdy axe. The collection of sticks was tied in a bundle on his back, so that his one good arm was free to chop and collect firewood.

Relaxing his stance but not lowering his sword, the brave young knight spoke to the poor man with kindness in his voice. "No, the fault is mine, I did not mean to startle you," he said. "Who are you and what are you doing in these woods?"

"I am but a poor woodcutter," the man replied, still too scared to move, his one right arm frozen above his head. "And these woods are my home."

The brave knight looked the woodcutter over once again. The axe tucked in the man's belt was sharp and had a large head but it was hardly any match for the perfectly balanced sword that the knight had. In comparison, it could barely be called a weapon. Especially when wielded by a one-armed man.

In a fight, the woodcutter would need to draw and strike using just one hand. Made all the more difficult since it was tucked so tightly into the man's belt. Having only his right arm, the woodcutter's balance would be compromised. The knight's training had taught him that with each swing the man would need to adjust his footing, which would have made his attacks slow and easy to dodge. Without the use of both hands, an opponent would not be able to attack and defend at the same time, as the knight could with a sword and shield. Also, while swinging the axe one-handed, an attacker would lack the power to deliver much more than a glancing blow. Against someone like the knight, who was wearing his polished steel breastplate over a coat of iron chain mail, a one-armed man with a woodcutter's axe would never even be able to draw blood.

Having assessed the situation, as he had been taught, the knight put his sword back in its scabbard and waved for the man to approach. The old woodcutter lowered his hand and took a few timid steps forward. Keeping his distance from the stranger, the man stopped and pointed to the stream saying, "That river is poisoned. But I have a water-skin with me here. I'm happy to share if you are in need."

Keeping his eyes on the knight, the man reached down very slowly to retrieve a large waterskin from the ground and held it out to the knight. The knight smiled, stepped confidently to the man, and took a long drink. "In order to find clean water you would need to travel much farther north," the man explained. "There used to be a very wide bridge farther upstream, but once long ago, a team of horses was lost when the bridge collapsed. Ever since that day, the water downstream from the broken bridge has been poisoned and everyone who drinks from it is killed."

The knight looked from the stranger to the stream and back again. In the growing darkness of the forest, it was impossible to see much of the water. But the knight imagined the rotting bodies of horses lying just under the surface of the water. "Thank you, kind sir," he said. "I am in your debt, and fortunate that we have met when we did."

The poor old woodcutter shook the knight's hand and said, "And I am fortunate," then he looked from the knight to his sword then to his horse and back to the knight, "that we met as friends and not on the battlefield." The knight laughed loud and long, confident in his strength and bravery.

The woodcutter pointed farther upstream and said, "I have a small camp, a short walk from here, where there is shelter and the water is clean. If you would join me, I'd be happy for the company and keen to learn what brings a knight such as yourself so deep into these woods." Needing a place to rest for the night, the young man agreed and followed the woodcutter to his camp.

They arrived well after the sun had set. By the time they stopped, the young knight could barely see the ground before his feet. To his embarrassment, he stumbled several times as they wound through the trees. The woodcutter had no trouble navigating the forest in the dark. Having lived there his whole life, he knew it as well as any other beast of the forest. To the young knight, it appeared that the man had special senses, like a wolf that can track its prey even in the darkest of nights.

The woodcutter had made a temporary camp in a small grove by a stream. Large boulders sheltered the pair from the cold winds that were blowing from the east, and within minutes the woodcutter had made a roaring fire. He then placed a small pot of water beside the fire to boil.

The knight busied himself tending to his horse and stripping off his armour. When he was done he joined the woodcutter by the fire and they shared the woodcutter's meagre meal of dried meat and fresh berries.

After they had eaten, the woodcutter set the pot of boiling water aside to cool and removed his tunic. The stump that was the remainder of his left arm was covered with a homemade bandage and held in place with a ripped piece of cloth that crossed his chest and was tied in a knot under his right arm. The woodcutter turned the severed limb away from the knight and grimaced while he peeled the bandage off and laid it on the ground. If the knight was honest with himself, he hadn't seen very much blood. He had heard the tales from the older knights in the king's court about grizzly injuries and gruesome deaths on the battlefield. He knew that one of the castle guards had lost a hand in battle, but that injury was old and healed. This was not.

While there was only a small spot of dried blood on the bandage, the cloth was soiled by the wound. Dark blotches appeared on the bandage where the wound was seeping. The dark grey stains and clear rings left behind by the puss from the wound made the knight think that the wound was infected. He understood why the woodcutter was treating the injury with such care; if the infection spread and turned to a fever, it could kill the old man.

The knight watched as the woodcutter took a small patch of clean cloth and dipped it in the steaming water. The woodcutter gasped through clenched teeth as the hot water touched the wound. With his body turned away from the fire, the young knight couldn't see the wound, though he tried to picture it clean and healed, similar to that of the castle guard. But instead, his mind conjured a ragged and torn piece of flesh hanging from the man's shoulder. The knight's stomach turned and he had no choice but to look away or be sick.

The old man worked in silence, cleaning and re-dressing the wound. After applying a fresh bandage and the torn cloth that held it in place, he began washing the old bandage in what was left of the boiled water. Repeatedly dunking the piece of cloth and rubbing the stains with the thumb of his right hand eventually got the sickly blotches of grey out of the cloth. It was the woodcutter who broke the uncomfortable silence. "It was an accident," he said, knowing that the young knight's eyes had been on him since he sat down. "It is kind of you to not inquire," he continued, "but it was just an accident nothing more."

The knight replied, "That pleases me to hear. I was worried that you had been attacked by an animal in these woods. It is a dangerous place. An old man like you would be safer in the city."

The mention of the city seemed to upset the wood-cutter as the knight saw the corner of his mouth curl in a slight snarl before relaxing back to a straight line on the man's creased face. The old man spoke, obviously trying to contain himself. "No, I would not be safer," he said. "I am safest in these woods. It was an accident. I should have been more cautious. I was not being careful, and it was costly." Then, looking directly at the young knight, meaning to end the conversation, he said again, "It was an accident and nothing more."

The old man settled down on the ground across the fire from the knight and asked what had brought the knight so deep into the woods.

The knight explained that he was sent by the king himself. His quest was to kill the monster that had been terrorizing the farms along the southern edge of the forest. "It comes only on the darkest nights," he said. "It needs to hunt when there is no moon or stars in the sky. That is part of its pact with the devil, that it can never be seen by human eyes. As long as it follows this one rule, then in return, the devil gives it powers beyond any other beast. The Woldger has the power to control men's minds, ruin crops, poison wells, and even bewitch other animals to do its bidding. That's how it has evaded our best hunters, until now." With that, he leaned against the boulder behind him and patted the sheathed sword sitting beside him.

The woodcutter stared across the fire at the young man and asked, "What can you tell me about this ... what did you call it?"

"The Woldger. It's an old word that the farmers say means demon," he said. "But all we know about it is from its attacks. Always on the darkest of nights, and it kills anything it wants. Sheep, cattle, chickens. Anything it comes across, it kills. It is only a matter of time before it attacks a person. So far it has eluded each of our hunting parties and all of our traps, except one."

The woodcutter got up from his spot and walked around the fire to sit beside the brave knight, intent on hearing his account of the trap that had caught the Woldger.

"In his wisdom, the king decided to have a series of traps set around a farm," he explained. "Along the fence where the sheep were kept, the royal hunters dug a shallow hole every few feet, and at the bottom of each, they placed a trap. It was a simple mechanism with a pressure plate and two sharp blades. If the Woldger stepped into the pit, the trap would slam shut, trapping the demon's foot. The king's soothsayers told the hunters when clouds would cover the night sky, and the king's men knew where to set the traps. Then the priests put holy water on each trap so that the devil would not be able to see them and warn the monster."

The woodcutter waited in silence for the brave young man to continue his tale.

"But alas," he said, "surely using some sort of witchcraft, the Woldger eluded our traps. In the morning the

47

royal hunters found that one trap had indeed been triggered; the blades had severed the demon's foot, but the Woldger had escaped. While the king's men wanted to bring it home as a trophy, the priests declared that it needed to be buried immediately. And to this day the farmers say that nothing will grow in the place where the Woldger's blood was spilt."

The woodcutter sat beside the fire, thinking about all he had just heard. Then he asked, "What did the foot look like?"

"In truth, I did not see it," admitted the knight. "But the king's hunters say that it was huge and fierce. Bigger than that of any wolf, with five claws, each as long as an eagle's talons. It was covered in coarse grey hair and matted with the dried blood of a thousand men. The priests say that when the holy water touched the paw it started to smoke, and before the hole was filled, they could see the ground opening up beneath it as the devil summoned his servant back to hell." The brave young knight quickly crossed himself before continuing his tale. "It is for these reasons that the king has sent his bravest knight to destroy the Woldger. And I will. No matter how long it takes, I will search these woods for the beast and I will end its evil once and for all."

The woodcutter spent a long time sitting in silence staring at the fire before he spoke. When he did he was solemn and stern. "I know where the Woldger is," he said. The young knight leapt to his feet. While he would never admit it, he was starting to lose faith, wondering if he would ever be able to finish his quest. The young knight ran to his horse and began to make ready the weapons and armour that he had carefully put away. "Come, let us away," he shouted to the old man.

"We must not leave right now," the woodcutter said. "There is much that I must tell you about the creature you hunt. Besides, you do not want to face this challenge in the darkness of night. You must wait till dawn."

The knight let out a deep breath to calm himself and said, "Again, I am grateful for your learned counsel. You are right. I would be wise to wait until dawn. It is on dark nights like tonight that Satan grants the Woldger its unnatural powers."

"Yes," said the old man after staring at the knight for a moment. "Come sit by the fire and I will tell you what I can to help your hunt. But be warned, although you are clearly very brave, this is a dangerous task."

The two companions spoke well into the night, with the woodcutter laying out a detailed plan for the knight. He was to ride half a day north where he would come to a sheer cliff of black stone. There, he would leave his horse and armour behind. Then he would cover his weapon with the holy water he had been given by the priests and, taking only his sword, he would scale the cliff. When he reached the top, hopefully before sunset, he would find a deep cave at the top of the cliff. Then, without hesitation, he was to charge into the cave. He would run into the Woldger's lair and hope to take it by surprise. The knight would never be able to sneak up on the creature, this was no frightened rabbit hiding under a thornbush. The wise woodcutter pointed out very clearly that the knight's only hope was to rush in, strike fast, and remember that the king's blessing was upon him.

The young knight agreed to follow the plan but added that he would leave at sunrise and he would ride hard in order to give himself as much daylight as possible to face the monster. Therefore avoiding the darkness that gives his prey its supernatural powers.

The two companions slept little, with one or both of them getting up often during the night to check the position of the moon or stare off to the east, looking for any sign of the rising sun. By the time the sun started to peek over the tops of the trees, the knight was already packed and climbing onto his horse. The woodcutter had given the knight the remainder of his food and wished him well, reminding him of the most important parts of the plan. "Ride straight north, head for the cliff as soon as you see it," he said. "When you reach the top, don't hesitate, just charge. That is your only chance."

The brave young knight thanked him for his wisdom and generosity and rode north, leaving the camp before the first rays of sunlight made the forest floor.

The knight guided his horse through the forest, painstakingly picking out a path between the trees and doing his best to keep his direction due north. However, the forest was so thick and the trees were so tall that he was almost at the base of the cliff before he saw it. By the time he tied up his horse and removed his armour, it was just before noon. Being sure to follow the instruction of the kindly old man, the young knight poured the holy water on his sword and even saved a few precious drops to pour on his head, then began his climb.

While the cliff face was huge and sheer, the climb was manageable for the strong young man. Years of rain and wind had left behind countless cracks, holes, and crevices from the forest floor to the top of the cliff. About halfway up there was even a thin ledge where the knight could rest and catch his breath. While he was disappointed he had not thought to bring some drinking water on his climb, he was happy to have left his armour behind. The added weight would have made summitting the black rock impossible. His armoured shoes, called sabatons in the king's court, would have never fit in the cracks and holes in the rock. But barefoot the brave young knight was able to wedge his feet into the tiny crevices of the sheer black cliff. The old woodcutter was wise to tell the knight to leave his armour behind.

Granted, he would rather be facing the Woldger wearing his shining silver armour and carrying his shield, but none of that would matter if he had to face the beast in the forest on a moonless night. The woodcutter was right, he needed to strike when the monster was most vulnerable. A direct attack on the beast's home was the only option. He peered down to the forest floor to see his armour. It was carefully hidden under a large low fern. Beside the fern, his horse was relaxing in the shade, munching on a tuft of grass.

A quick glance at the sun as it continued its unrelenting path through the sky reminded the knight that the protection of the sun would not last forever, and so he continued climbing. He was almost at the top of the cliff, and thanks to his training, he knew that he would be most vulnerable when he reached the summit. When he got to the top, the Woldger may be waiting for him. The devil may have given the monster a warning, or the Woldger may have used its evil magic to bewitch another animal to spy on the knight. Either way, if the Woldger knew of the knight's approach, he would be defenceless when he got to the top. He'd be clinging to the top of a sheer cliff with his only weapon sheathed on his hip. One swipe from the beast's foul paw could send the brave knight plummeting to his death before he even had a chance to draw his sword. He reminded himself to be cautious and prayed that the good fortune he'd had since meeting the woodcutter yesterday would continue when he reached the top.

When he was one long reach from the top of the cliff, he paused and grabbed a closer hold. Setting his feet against a large crack to his left, he was able to push himself up and lift his head above the grass covering the top. He was vulnerable but poised to lower his head back down in case the demon was waiting for him. But he need not have worried. There was no Woldger to be seen.

The summit was a large flat plateau covered in grass and shrubs. Directly across from where the knight had climbed up was a dark cave. Only the first few steps into the mouth of the cave were visible. The cave appeared to descend quickly into the top of the cliff, diving down into the earth. The knight knew instantly that the woodcutter was correct, this was the lair of the Woldger.

After surveying the peak and deeming it safe, he pulled himself up onto the top of the cliff. The climb was gruelling and the brave young knight would have preferred to rest, but he remembered what the woodcutter had told him about charging the beast and he drew his sword. His lungs were burning and his muscles ached but he pulled his sword to his hip and began to run to the mouth of the cave. Not knowing what awaited him, he had to rely on his training to guide him. He had his left arm out, poised to aid his balance or grapple with the beast if he had to. His knees were bent to help him lower his centre of gravity and give his opponent as small a target as possible. He was gaining speed, sprinting toward his destiny when he hit the sticks.

About a dozen. Thin, each between two and three feet long, lined up side by side, and covered with a scattering of green leaves. The leaves allowed the sticks to camouflage what they were covering: a hole about two feet deep that had been dug very recently. It contained a long sharpened stick, one end buried firmly in the earth, the other pointing straight up. The sharp end was there to impale the knight's foot, and it did much more than that.

With his attention focused on his form as he charged the Woldger's lair, he was running at full speed when he stepped on the sharpened spike. Before the brave knight had a chance to see the sticks and leaves that covered the hole, the spike was already through the bottom of his left foot. Running at a full sprint, his inertia was transferred from his stride across the ground down to the spike that waited for him. With that final forceful step, the sharpened stick was able to split the bones between the knight's foot and tear through the top of his foot. If the knight had been walking unaware, he would have impaled his foot. But with the force of his charge, the spike did not stop at his foot. As he fell into the perfectly placed hole, the spike continued upward toward his shin. The well-sharpened end lodged between the bones in his shin and came to rest just under the back of his knee.

The brave knight fell face down on the grass, pinned to the earth. Locked in place by the pain. Shackled by the wooden stake that went from his foot to his knee, he lay there in silence. Unable to move, his exhaustion and pain left him vulnerable on the ground face down as he waited for his foe to deal the fatal blow. He could imagine the creature approaching and the fatal bite that would be his end. Sharp fangs and powerful jaws would soon hit the back of his neck and end his suffering. Like a wolf killing a lamb, the Woldger would strike the back of his neck and sever his spine in a single bite.

But nothing came.

Eventually, the knight was able to raise his head off the ground. He was fighting to control his breathing. The pain made each inhale a painful ordeal, and with each exhale the knight had to fight to keep from losing the contents of his stomach.

Slowly and carefully, the knight tried to survey the area around him, but he was barely able to move. Anything more than lifting his head up would result in crippling pain radiating from his foot to his knee. He had to slide his face along the dirt to look left and right for his foe.

But there was nothing new to be seen. The Woldger had not emerged from its cave. There was nothing around him but the same small ferns and tufts of grass. Then the knight realized that the nothing around him included his sword. It was nowhere to be found. His only weapon was gone.

The knight knew he was defenceless. Wounded and pinned to the ground, he had no chance of completing his quest unless he could find his sword, but that would mean getting out of the trap. With a slow exhale he moved his hands down his left leg, he groped along his leg to confirm what the pain had already told him. The spike had skewered his foot, come out through the top, driven back into his shin and lodged itself deep in his left leg. As his fingers gingerly reached the back of his knee, he could feel the bulge of the point as it pushed out the skin just below his left knee. Taking a breath to try and calm himself, he resolved that he would have to free himself from the trap if he was to defeat the Woldger.

He braced his elbows on either side of the trap and wrapped his hands around his calf. His plan was to pull the leg up quickly, and hope that he did not faint from the pain. Unconscious on the ground, he would be nothing but food for the Woldger. The knight took a deep breath and prayed for strength when he heard a voice say, "I wouldn't do that if I were you."

The voice came from behind him, slightly farther back than he was able to see. "I'm sorry," the familiar voice said, "but if you pull the spike out, you will most certainly bleed to death in that hole." It was the voice of the kind old woodcutter. "You actually made it up the cliff much faster than I expected, I had to really rush to get that trap set before you got here. Good thing you decided to charge the cave or you might have noticed the hole." The knight's mind was churning, the pain made it impossible to understand what had happened.

"You left me no choice, really," said the woodcutter as he rounded the knight to his left, keeping his distance, although it was clear the knight was no threat, even to an old woodcutter with just one arm. "When you said you would destroy the — what did you call it? The Woldger, was it? When you said nothing would stop you, I knew what I had to do. Luckily, getting you to trust me wasn't that hard, but if I hadn't seen you about to drink from that poisoned stream, I don't know what I would have done to earn your confidence." As he spoke the woodcutter stepped around to where the knight could see him. As he circled the knight, he stretched his arm out in front and flexed the fingers on his one remaining hand.

"If you had come up here from the east," he said, "as I did, you would have found it much easier. In fact, you could have ridden your horse. Right up to the mouth of this cave, with all your shining armour and sharp weapons. I couldn't let that happen, so I told you of the cliff and the need to leave those things behind. Did it honestly never occur to you to ask if there was another way to the top of the cliff?" As the woodcutter spoke, he continued to stretch and flex his body. Twisting his neck like he was trying to work out some tense knot in his spine. When he did this, the knight thought he heard the sound of breaking bones. But that was probably only in his head.

The knight's mind was drowning in pain. He could hardly rely on it to tell him the truth. But he would have sworn that the woodcutter grew taller as he walked in a circle. That was impossible. But yet, as he rounded the knight, it looked like he was growing taller with every step.

The brave young knight tried to think back to his training, but all he could think of was that he had a mission to complete. Which he said to the woodcutter, still hoping for his help.

"I have been sent on a quest," he said. "I am a knight of the royal court sent by the king himself."

"You are a fool sent by a fool!" the woodcutter growled from behind the knight. His voice was a deep roar. He now sounded nothing like the wise old man who had counselled the young knight beside the fire yesterday.

"Your king knows nothing of this forest," he shouted as he rounded the wounded knight once again, continuing to flex and stretch as we walked. The knight would have sworn that the old man had grown, both taller and more broad. "He knows nothing of the beauty of this forest. The natural order that exists. He doesn't understand that here he is not the king. Here he is just another animal," he stopped pacing and squatted down in front of the young knight.

"And you. You know nothing about what you are hunting."

The knight stared in wonder at the old man's face. The woodcutter's jaw was being contorted and twisted. The bones were cracking and breaking as he stretched out his chin and gnashed his teeth. His teeth were growing, too. The knight saw that each time the old man opened his mouth, his teeth looked longer and sharper. Not like a man's mouth, more like an animal's jaws.

Exhaustion threatened to overwhelm the knight. His tired hands clutched handfuls of grass as he hoped to steady himself. His breaths were slow sips of air as the pain in his left leg threatened to strip away his consciousness. He tried to defend his quest. "The Woldger is a servant of evil sent to plague the nearby farms," he said.

The woodcutter stretched his right arm out and crawled toward the knight, slowly closing in on the trapped man, and said, "It is an animal, and it behaves as all animals do. When it is hungry, it eats. When it is threatened, it protects its territory. When it is wounded in a trap, it will chew off its own leg to free itself." The knight could barely understand what the woodcutter was saying. His mind was scattered by the pain, blood was pouring from his left leg and he would soon faint.

The woodcutter sat back on his haunches and watched as the colour drained from the knight's face and his head began to fall to the ground. Catching the knight's head as it dropped, the old man's hand covered the knight's mouth and his fingernails dug into the knight's cheeks. With the pain the knight woke up, his face was a sickly white as blood ran out of his body and filled the hole he was trapped in. There was nothing he could do but listen.

"Do you understand that?" he roared in the knight's face. "A brief lapse in judgment, one small accident, and the animal is forced to chew off its own leg." The wood-cutter dropped the knight's face and, too weak to hold up his own head, he fell face down in the grass. Unable to stop himself from lunging forward in the trap, the spike in his leg moved and tore even deeper into his calf. Too weak to scream, the knight lay face down crying into the grass.

"One mistake, made out of hunger, and your trap cost it an arm. Driven to the city by hunger and it had to chew off its own arm! Do you think you could do that? In order to survive, with all your bravery, could you now cut off that leg to free yourself?"

The knight looked up at the old man, not to answer; he knew he would never be able to free himself from this trap. But he wanted to show his bravery. He would face his final foe with his eyes open. He looked back at the woodcutter and tried to meet the old man's stare.

"Everything that you know about this creature is wrong," the woodcutter growled in the knight's face. "It cannot control minds. It cannot ruin crops, poison wells, or bewitch animals." It was then, just for an instant, the knight was able to focus his vision long enough to notice the woodcutter's eyes. No longer the kind eyes of an old man, they were drawn and thin, yellow like a wolf's eyes, with the deep blackness of a nighttime hunter.

"You know nothing of this creature," the woodcutter said as he continued to twist and writhe. "You didn't even know that sometimes it can take the shape of man."

MAKING PLANS FOR HALLOWEEN

WHAT ARE WE DOING FOR Halloween? I'm so glad you asked. Normally we just head out in our little groups, roaming the neighbourhood looking to get as many as we can.

But this year we are going to do things differently. This year I called everyone together at my house and I told them my plan.

I laid out the map I had made of the neighbourhood, and everyone crowded around to take a look. One of the younger ones was obviously too excited and shouted out, "Oh, this is going to be great, I'm going to eat till I burst!"

I smiled at him and waited for the group to quiet down. As the oldest one there, I had done this more times than anyone, and it was my plan, so I was in charge.

"There will be plenty for everyone," I told them. "But the only way we can get them all is if we work together.

"First, a few rules for anyone who is new here.

"We don't start till after the sun sets, by then all the babies and the parents are gone, and they just get in the way anyway."

I tried to make eye contact with some of the young ones to make sure they were listening. This was important and I didn't want them to miss any details.

"And you have to keep up. If you fall behind because you have a peg leg, or an eye patch, then you are on your own," I said.

"We only get to do this one night of the year. So we have to make it count." The crowd quieted down, and I knew they were starting to take it all seriously.

"And finally, and most importantly, stick to the plan. Alone, we can have a good night, there is enough out there for everyone. But if we stick to the plan, we can get them all."

Some of them were drooling at this point. I paused for a moment. I knew what everyone was imagining. They were all thinking of bags and bags full to bursting being hauled down into this basement. Bags so heavy that they could barely lift them. So heavy that they would have to drag them, bouncing down the stairs, into my basement. This table covered with piles and everyone here getting to pick through and savour their favourite pieces.

"So here is where we begin." I pointed to the map, to the intersection of Oak and Elm, just up the hill from the graveyard. I knew from experience there would be lots in the area but I wanted to make sure it didn't get too busy.

"You guys," I said as I pointed to a pack of newbies hovering by the door. "This is your neighbourhood, so it's your job to keep an eye on the crowds. Check in regularly and if the crowds get really big, I want to know. At the end of the night, when you think you've seen the last of them, head back here for the feast." When I said "feast," everyone let out a little giggle.

I didn't laugh. I wanted them to know I was serious but my stomach was starting to growl as I talked about the plan.

"It's going to be dark," I said loudly. The laughing stopped immediately. "I want you to use that to your advantage." I directed their attention to the map on the table and pointed to the place where Oak Street met Elm Street. "As the crowds gather here, stretch those shadows out wherever you can. Everywhere that there isn't a porch light or a street light, you should be making things as dark as you can. Do it slowly so that they won't notice. Maybe just break a porch light here or there. But make sure that the neighbourhood gets darker and darker as the night goes on."

A group of veterans all nodded in agreement. They not only knew what to do, they knew the effect it would have.

I traced my bony finger along Green Street. "When they get here, that's when I want some of you moving in the shadows," I said. "Remember not to be seen. We don't want to reveal ourselves. We just want them to notice some quick movements out of the corners of their eyes. Something that they can't identify. But something that they know is there."

I scanned the room. I saw nothing but smiling faces looking back, they knew just what to do.

"Here we want them to turn down Robinson Street," I said pointing to a long laneway that led toward the graveyard. "That way we can separate them from the larger crowds. We want small groups of five or six kids. So here is where I want the wind to hit them."

I pointed to the two brothers over my shoulder. They were very old and very powerful.

"It will seem to come out of nowhere." I couldn't help but smile while I talked. "A shrieking wind that shakes the dead branches of the trees and blows the last few leaves onto the ground. I want it sharp and cold as it rolls down the backs of their necks, freezing their skin. Instinctively, they will turn their backs to the wind and head our way. They will be walking toward us, not really paying attention to where they are going, huddled together against the wind."

I placed a finger halfway down Robinson Street, right where a long but gentle hill starts.

"As they continue toward the cemetery, they'll start to notice fewer houses, which means fewer lights," I said as I scanned the room. "When they get to the bottom of the hill, they will be surprised to find it is very dark, and they are very alone." The crowd erupted with laughter, it was a high cackle that echoed off the bare stone walls of the dark basement.

"We need them to turn east, toward this place," I said as I pointed to where my house was on the map. "You, I need a scream, right here!" I said to the creature beside me. His black cloak hid his face but I knew what he was. He was hungry and he was ready to hunt. "A powerful and piercing scream that overwhelms them. They will cover their ears only to realize that the scream is coming from inside their own minds and they will run to get away from the sound."

I saw one of the young ones looking nervously around the room. I was expecting this.

"And at this point, there might be some who are too scared and want to go home," I said, trying to sound reassuring. "But that's okay, we want them to be afraid. But what we don't want is for them to convince anyone in their group to go home. So what do we do?" I asked the group, knowing that none of them had the answer. But I did.

"We scare them so much that they can't even talk," I explained. The whole group smiled at the idea, some with bright clean teeth, some with fangs, some with rotted holes where mouths used to be.

"When you find that scared little kid looking into the darkness and you look right back," I said, "let them see blood-red eyes filled with hunger and hatred. Show them eyes that belong to a beast that is waiting for them to look away.

"They will panic.

"They will run.

"And I will give them somewhere to run to."

Not a sound came from the others in the room. "They will look down the street," I said, "and they will see this house. But they won't see a condemned house where a teenager died. They won't see a burned-out shack where a body was dumped to hide a murder a long time ago.

"No, they will see a warm and welcoming home, with soft lights and a wide-open door that tells their terrified little minds that they will be safe inside. But of course, that's where we will be waiting."

I leaned back in my chair, one ragged arm outstretched on the map. Mostly bones held together by tendons and bits of meat. Most of the cloth from my jacket rotted away years ago. Barely enough now to see the bloodstain from where the knife went into my chest so long ago.

I smiled and said, "And that's how we do it, one group at a time until this basement is full. Heaps and piles all over and everyone gets to pick out their favourite pieces."

There were cheers from the crowd, a chorus of ghouls and ghosts who were ready for the feast.

I was reminded that some of them have not eaten all year.

It made me want to go over the rules once more.

"Remember, we wait until dark, our powers are strongest when the sun is gone.

"We only get to do this once a year, it is our one chance to feed, and if we work together … we can get them all."

So that's the plan: one hand-drawn map and a room full of hungry ghosts.

So, while you and your friends are planning your Halloween route, so are we.

While you're thinking about where to go and what will taste the best, so are we.

Plan your route, bring your flashlight if it makes you feel better, tell yourself that you won't be scared.

It won't matter.

'Cause this year we've got a plan, and we're going to work together to get you all.

THE STRANGE GRAVE OF MIKEY DUNBAR, NUMBER 2

THERE IS A STRANGE GRAVE far north of here. It sits beside an ancient pub, tucked amongst some trees, just outside a tiny town that sits hidden along a rocky shore. In the summer you will find all the windows open and a cool breeze that blows in from the sea. In the winter the windows are covered in frost and the crooked chimney on the roof is constantly letting out wisps of smoke from the small fireplace inside.

The grave has no name, no dates, just the words *buy me a drink* carved in the smooth black tombstone. Yes, it's a tombstone, not a gravestone. A gravestone stands upright to mark a grave. A tombstone is a thick stone slab that lies flat on the ground and covers a tomb. It would have been very heavy, extremely expensive, and therefore only ever used for someone of great importance. It has to make you wonder, who would be buried beside a pub? And why is there no name?

Maybe the strangest thing about this grave is the tradition that surrounds it. Each and every customer at the pub takes the last sip of each drink and pours it on the grave. Why? Another good question.

The bar's owner, a full-time bartender and almost full-time drinker, will tell a tale of a curse on the bar. It is the story of an old hermit named Mikey Dunbar who came in one night back when the owner's great-great-grandfather ran the place. Mikey lived alone in a shack outside of town, only came into town rarely and had never come to the bar before. Mikey had no family in town and only came into town to collect his mail a few times a year. In fact, the mail was the only reason anyone knew his name.

On the night of Mikey Dunbar's visit, the great-great-grandfather of the bartender was surprised to see the hermit walk through the door, but welcomed the old man to the pub. However, instead of sitting down and ordering, the poor man went from customer to customer and begged for a free drink. The only words the poor man said as he roamed from table to table were "buy me a drink." While everyone in the pub turned the poor soul down, the great-great-grandfather took pity on the man and gave him a whiskey on the house. Sometimes the bartender adds a hot meal to the story to further illustrate his family's generous nature.

When the hermit was done his drink, and his meal depending on the version being told, he thanked the barkeep and went to leave, but as he reached the exit he turned to the crowd and told them that because of their greed and lack of charity, they would be cursed and only the kindly bartender would escape a terrible fate.

The patrons mocked and laughed at the poor man despite the desperate pleas from the generous bartender to show some kindness to the man. Then, with a nod to the bartender for his generosity, the poor man left the pub, walked to the edge of the property, and dropped dead in the very place where his grave now stands. That night, every single one of those unrepentant customers was burned alive in a series of unexplained house fires.

In the bartender's tale, each of the homes of the patrons was consumed by fire. But the flames never damaged any other homes. Not a single ash or spark landed anywhere else but on the houses of the selfish pub-goers. In the cases of those who had family, only the greedy customers died. In each incident, the other family members were miraculously able to escape the fire unharmed.

However, in each case, no body was ever recovered. The bartender would say that the cause of the fires could never be explained and the reason no corpses were recovered was that the fires were set by the devil himself. Satan had heard the hermit's curse and had personally taken the souls of the townsfolk straight to hell.

The next day the pub hosted a memorial to the victims of the fire and to the hermit. The generous pub owner had paid to have them all entombed together. He believed that since fate had connected their deaths, they should be together forever in the afterlife. At the end of the night, the bartender led the patrons outside to the grave so they could toast the deceased. Sometimes it's a free round of drinks from the benevolent pub owner, again depending on the version being told. In any version of the story, the pub owner told the gathered mourners that they poured the last of their drinks on the grave in the hope that the spirits would stay at rest and that the living would remember the crucial lesson of generosity for their fellow man.

Whenever the bartender is telling his tale to someone who is new to the bar, he will finish with a grim warning that the newcomer heed the tradition, or they may risk angering the powerful spirits who are buried just outside the door. Then he explains that it is a tradition that he always observes, no matter how bad the weather or how late it is or how tired he is. He has never forgotten to pour out the last sip of his drink. Never. He will then say, "'Tis better to give a sip to the ghost than to end up as one."

The more jaded patrons will point out that, for the bartender, it was a great way to sell a little more booze, and maybe get a bigger tip. Plus, whenever the bartender gets to tell his tale to one of the few tourists that visit during the summer months, they usually come back again, and often with friends. Before the end of their visit, most tourists make another visit to the "strange grave," and will excitedly ask the bartender to tell the tale to the group of friends they brought along.

They will sit and drink and then pour the last sip of their drink onto the grave of Mikey Dunbar, knowing that every word of the tale is true.

OUR LITTLE PUMPKIN PATCH

KEN WAS A GRUMPY OLD man. Never rude, but he rarely smiled and never talked. He'd work all day at his little booth at the farmers' market and never say a single word. Each weekend hundreds of people would walk past, dozens would stop and buy his vegetables, and he'd conduct each transaction with just a few nods and grunts. He'd sell everything he had each and every weekend and never say a word.

Luckily, his wife talked enough for the both of them. Dot was a plump and pleasant old lady. She'd chat with each and every person who walked by their booth at the farmers' market. It didn't matter if they were customers or just passing by, she loved to chat. If they were customers, she'd chat them up about the weather and why it's looking like a good season for corn. If they were just passing by, she'd offer them a cherry to sample, which would usually turn that passerby into a customer.

She baked cookies and brought them to the farmers' market, too. Not to sell, just to give away whenever kids came by. She'd spot a mom with a stroller or a dad pulling a wagon full of kids and then, quick as a flash, she'd grab her tin of homemade cookies and head into the crowd to offer the kids some chocolate chip cookies that she had made just that morning. She'd say things to them like "sweetie" and "dearie" and "you look just like an angel."

The parents never said no. Dot was a chubby-cheeked, grey-haired little old lady. Only about five feet tall and probably just as wide. Each Sunday at the farmers' market, she wore a red-and-white checkered apron over her cornflower-blue dress. She was the perfect picture of the sweet little old lady, and every parent who looked at her chubby pink face knew that they had nothing to worry about.

Ken was the opposite, not just in personality but in appearance, too. About as thin as a man could be, with hunched shoulders and long arms that were always crossed in front of his chest. If he wasn't silently bagging produce for a customer, he was as far back from the vegetable stand as he could be. Leaning against the bumper of their old truck with his arms crossed and head down. Unlike his wife's skin, which was pink and plump, his was wrinkled, tanned, and tough. Years of labour in the fields had left his skin dry and worn; years of digging in the dirt and fixing old tractors meant that his hands were permanently stained. Everything about him, his appearance, his posture, the permanent frown on his creased face, said he did not want to talk. But that never stopped people from trying, after all, at the farmers' market he was a bit of a celebrity.

Every year at the end of the season, there was a huge festival and Ken's pumpkins were always the biggest attraction. Literally. The market hosted a pumpkin growing contest and Ken had grown the biggest one for as long as anyone could remember. On the last Sunday before the end of the summer break, before the kids would start another year of school, the county would host a gigantic fall festival. There were carnival rides and ice cream trucks. Lots of games so you could win a stuffed toy for your sweetheart and even a dunk tank that raised money for the volunteer firefighters. Farmers from all over would travel to the "fall fair" to show off their best, and maybe win a prize. The best bull or the best apple pie could win a blue ribbon from the mayor, but only the largest pumpkin would win you a cash prize. Each person who entered a pumpkin in the contest had to pay a five-dollar fee. Whoever had the heaviest pumpkin won half the money, the other half of the pot went to the local 4-H club. But that money didn't matter. The real money came from selling the seeds.

Each year at the fair, the farmer who won the blue ribbon and the envelope of five-dollar bills would sell the seeds from the previous year's winning pumpkin. If you won one year, you could charge one hundred dollars for a small package of seeds. But since Ken had won for more than a dozen years in a row, he sold his seeds for five hundred dollars for just three seeds. The next year he would charge even more. Each year he won the contest, each year the price went up, and each year he would sell out of seeds.

Not that everyone used Ken and Dot's seeds. Many of the local farmers had their own pumpkin seeds that they used. Picking the seeds from their biggest pumpkins each year and planting them again in the hope of one day growing the biggest one at the fair and then getting rich selling their own seeds.

Some were just in it for fun. There was no shortage of fathers and sons who would join in the contest. They would grow a large pumpkin and bring it to the fall fair in a wheelbarrow. They usually gave it a cool nickname like "The Beast" or "Big Bob" and the kid would get an overenthusiastic cheer from the crowd when the mayor read the official weight.

Once there was even a pair of teenagers who got caught cheating in the contest. They brought in a surprisingly small pumpkin, but when it was put on the scale it was clearly the heaviest. A brief investigation revealed that they had stuck steel BBs in the pumpkin to weigh it down. This incident led to the new practice of running a magnet over every pumpkin in the contest. If the magnet sticks, your pumpkin is disqualified.

Once in a while, the seed-buyers were from out of town. They'd hear about Ken and his monster-sized pumpkins and travel to the fall fair just to try and grab some of the special seeds. Most of them planned to win the pumpkin contest back wherever they lived. Hoping to become a local celebrity with a big pumpkin of their own. Most of them would also try to get any inside information out of Ken. Of course, they would get nothing from him. Dot always liked to chat with the out-of-towners, and that's exactly what happened at the last fall fair.

The contest was over. Ken had won again and he was handing out seeds and collecting cash. The locals were always courteous. They'd congratulate him on another win and usually add a good-natured challenge about topping him next year. This year's pumpkin was smaller than the record-setter he had grown the year before so there were plenty of people who laughed and told him he was slipping or asked why his pumpkin was so "puny" this year. He never really responded and the locals never expected him to.

It was one of the out-of-towners who tried to chat up Ken. "Hey old timer," he said as he picked up a packet containing three pumpkin seeds. "I hear you're the king bee around here. What's your secret? Are these seeds magic or something?" The man turned the package over in his hands, just a small brown envelope with the cover taped shut.

The man had on boots, jeans, and a red plaid jacket. It was the uniform of a farmer, and every man with a stand at the market that day was wearing pretty much the exact same thing. But this guy was wearing it all wrong. The boots were brown leather, but not steel toe, plus they were clean. For the farmers at the fall fair, even their shoes for church were dirty. His jeans were rolled up at the hem; the working men would never do that. They had the common sense to just buy the correct sized jeans, and if their legs were too short, something that wasn't a concern for Ken, they'd just hike them up with a belt. Even if his clothes had been right, one look at the man's hands and Ken could tell he wasn't a farmer. Smooth, manicured, and clean. He was an outsider. "Tell me, what's your soil pH level like?"

the stranger asked. "You in the six, six-and-a-half range?" This guy knew his stuff — he was no farmer, but he knew his stuff.

Ken barely even acknowledged that the man was speaking. He simply nodded at the man's questions while serving the locals who wanted to buy his giant pumpkin seeds. They would approach, say something brief about his win, hand over the money, take the seeds, and leave without ever getting or expecting a word out of Ken.

When the stranger didn't get any response, Dot stepped in. "Oh, you aren't going to get anything out of that old sourpuss," she said as she stepped in between her husband and the stranger. Her sweet smile instantly won over the stranger, as it did with everyone she met. "I'm the one you want to talk to, but I'll warn you, you won't get any secrets out of me." Then she added a laugh; it was a young girl's laugh and it made her somehow even more adorable.

"Oh, I was just wondering about the pH levels in your soil." The stranger turned to her with a smile to match hers. "Do you know what your levels are like? How often do you test?" he asked.

"Well, I don't think we've ever tested the soil for pH." She turned to her husband. "Have we ever tested the soil for pH?" He, of course, just continued serving customers at the vegetable stand in silence. She had gotten the answer she expected and turned back to the inquisitive man and said, "I'll be honest with you, friend, I'm not sure if I really know what a pH level is."

Like most knowledgeable people, the man was happy to explain and at the same time show off his intelligence.

"The pH level refers to how acidic the soil is. Most of the soil around here is in the eight-to-nine range, but the research shows that for pumpkins the pH level should be between six and seven."

"Well, I can't tell you much about the acid in the soil." She gave a faint smile, seemingly embarrassed by her lack of knowledge. "But I know the soil is rich and dark and slightly red. That's most likely a little bit of clay mixed in. The land has been in my family for six generations." Then she pointed to the packets of seeds on the table and raised her voice just slightly to make sure she was heard by the small crowd gathered at the vegetable stand. "And we have always had the best pumpkins." There were several nodding heads amongst the group of locals who were picking through the cobs of corn or waiting for their turn to buy seeds.

The stranger was unsatisfied and changed his line of questioning. "What about the water?" he asked. "Are you on well water or municipal water? What about calcium in the water, have you had the calcium levels tested?"

She smiled her usual chubby-cheeked grandmother smile, happy that she could answer this question. "We're on well water, of course," she explained. "The farm is well outside of the town limits, they won't ever run city water pipes out to our place and if they did I can't say I'd let them. Ken's daddy and my daddy dug that well themselves and it's served our family every day since then." She then copied Ken's pose and crossed her arms. Only difference was, she was smiling.

The stranger laughed despite himself, her frank-but-friendly, down-home country charm had won him over and he handed over his cash in exchange for his packet of three seeds. After Dot had stuffed the small pile of bills into the pocket of her apron, she offered the man one of the homemade cookies that she usually reserved for kids. He loved it.

"Wow, these are good," he said in between bites.

"Now that secret I can tell you," she said and leaned in to whisper to the man. "Too much butter. My rule for baking is easy: if you think you've added too much butter, then you've added just enough."

The stranger grinned with a mouth full of cookie.

"So where are you from? What's your name?" she asked. I know you ain't from here; I know you ain't no farmer."

"Is it that obvious?" he said, laughing. "My name's Charles. I'm a chemistry professor at the university. I specialize in agricultural chemistry. I stopped for a bite outside of town and the people at the next table were talking about the fair and your pumpkins. I had time to kill so I thought I'd check it out."

"You hear that, Ken? We're famous," she said, turning to her husband and smiling. He reacted to the news the same way he did everything, with silence.

"I thought your seeds could make an interesting research project. That's why I was asking so many questions about the chemistry, for my students," he said, apologizing and explaining at the same time.

"It's a long way to the university, you came all this way for lunch? And some pumpkin seeds?" she asked, but her sweet voice and sweet smile didn't make it seem like she was intruding.

"Not exactly, I'm supposed to be on my way back from a teaching conference. I ... I thought I'd take a detour," he explained.

"Then shouldn't you be getting back, dearie? Someone's got to be worried sick about you." Her plump fingers touched his elbow as she reached over the rickety wooden table that acted as their counter at the farmers' market.

"Nah," he replied. "Nobody's waiting for me at home." Saying it out loud made him a little sad so he decided to change his tone. "One of the great things about being single is that I can take detours and meet interesting people," he said, then he smiled and patted her hand.

"I'll tell you what," she said as she nodded her head to the right and walked off toward the front of the pickup truck and away from the small crowd at the vegetable stand. The stranger followed her. When she stopped she looked around briefly to be sure that they weren't being observed. "It's not the seeds," she confided in a whisper. "That's why we can sell the seeds and still never lose. It's all about the soil. There's something special in the soil. That's why we've kept the farm in my family for so long." She thought for a moment, looking down at the tips of her steel-toe boots poking out from under the hem of her dress. Then she looked up into Charles's eyes and smiled. "I'll tell you what. If you come out to the farm, I'll show you exactly what makes our soil special, maybe help with your research project."

He was excited and overeager for the invite. "That's fantastic, can we go now? I mean, thank you," he said. He lowered his voice. "That's very generous of you. When would be a good time for a visit?"

She smiled her sweet grandmother's smile. "You can come by tonight after the market closes down. We usually eat a late supper on market days, so you can join us for supper if you'd like?"

"That would be wonderful," he said, although more interested in getting soil and water samples than food.

"Okay, Ken will take me home and I'll get things ready then he'll come back and get you," she said, then explained her reasoning. "The farm is pretty far off the beaten path. You'd never find it on your own."

"Thanks, I really appreciate this," he whispered and looked around to reassure himself that they weren't being watched. "See you tonight."

"Tonight," she said before quickly stepping over to her tin of homemade cookies and taking off the lid. "Have one more, dearie, in case you get hungry waiting for dinner."

He smiled, picked out a large one and headed off into the crowd.

By the time Ken showed up, the sun was almost gone and his was the only vehicle left in the market parking lot. Charles had been waiting for hours and was thinking about leaving when he saw Ken's old pickup coming down the road. Talkative as always, Ken made it a very quiet ride. Charles tried to make small talk. Said thanks for the invitation and the ride. Mentioned the lovely sunset and the warm summer breeze. Asked about Ken's family and how long they had been in the county. Each time the response was silence. Eventually, Charles decided to relax and enjoy the ride. The radio was playing a song called "Goodbye Earl." Charles had never heard it before but he liked it.

They rode in silence for a long while before pulling into an old farmstead. A huge spread of land surrounded the farm — acres and acres of recently harvested land waiting to be tilled and prepared for new crops next spring. A long gravel driveway led to a small white house and a large red barn. A mix of ancient and brand-new farm vehicles was spread out on the grass, filling the large space between the house and the barn. Dot waited in the huge open doorway of the barn, waving and smiling.

She retreated into the barn as Charles and her husband approached. Ken with his head down and Charles looking up at the fading pink sunset as it continued to sink behind the high peak of the huge barn roof. Charles walked into the spacious and mostly empty barn. The last of the summer crop had just been sold so all that was left in the barn was a cluttered workbench in the corner and a large blue tarp spread out on the floor. Charles noticed he was standing in the middle of the tarp just before he heard the gunshot. He heard it before he felt it. But by then he was already on his back.

He was staring up at the hayloft, trying to wrap his head around what had just happened. He looked down at his chest to see a number of dark-red blotches on his plaid jacket. He noted that the red stains were growing fast and they would soon connect into one big red blotch. He absent-mindedly wondered what would happen after that. A small voice in his head whispered, "You've been shot, get up, get up and run."

That's when Dot spoke. "Please don't get up, dearie. We really don't want you making a mess." She was walking up to where he lay on the blue tarp. As she walked she removed the spent shell from the shotgun and replaced it with a fresh one from her apron. She never even looked at the gun as she did it. She knew what she was doing, she was a farm girl after all. "It's not the pH or the calcium," she said.

The man bleeding on the blue tarp on the floor of the barn had no idea what she was talking about.

"The chemistry," she explained. "You asked about the pH levels in the soil and the amount of calcium in the well water. They've been tested and there's nothing special there. It's no different here than any of the other farms around."

The dark-red stains were now one stain and covered most of his chest. He thought he knew what she wanted to hear. "I won't say anything, I promise," he pleaded. "I'm not going to tell anyone." He started to cry as he pulled the packet of pumpkin seeds out of his front pocket and held them out to Dot. She smiled her sweet smile and said, "I know you're not going to tell anyone, sweetie."

"Please, please don't," he begged, though the pain and the fear made it hard to speak.

"I'm sorry, sweetie, but we need you here," she explained in her frank-but-friendly tone. "This land has been in my family for generations, and we've known its secret all along. It's the oxygen in the soil that makes the difference. And as a chemist, you know that hemoglobin transports oxygen in blood. My great-granddaddy said that they used to try this with pigs and cattle back in his day. But, you're an educated man, so you know that the big difference between human blood and animal blood is the amount of hemo-globin. Human blood has more hemoglobin, and —" she liked showing off her knowledge, especially to a man who thought he knew more than she did "— human males have more than females. So it has to be like this, it has to be you," she explained.

Charles started to feel faint, maybe from the blood loss, maybe from the realization that he was going to die in this barn. He needed to stall for time. "You're never going to get away with this," he croaked.

Her sweet smile turned to a sympathetic frown. "Oh, sweetie," she said, "of course we are. There's no one at home waiting for you, remember? It will be days or maybe weeks before the school starts looking for their absent employee. Then all they will find is your abandoned car in an empty parking lot, a parking lot no one saw you leave. There is nothing to point them to this place." She pointed to Ken, who walked to the workbench and retrieved a length of rope. He threw one end of the rope over the wooden beam above Charles's head. Then he took the other end and tied a tight knot around the bleeding man's ankles. "If they ask the other farmers about you, all anyone will be able to say is that they saw you buy seeds from us, we chatted, and you had a cookie. That's no more than what we did with dozens of other people at the market today."

Too weak to fight, all Charles could say was no. His blood had soaked through his clothes and was now starting to pool on the blue tarp under him.

Dot continued, speaking like she had no choice but to tell bad news to a good friend. "And if the police ever do come here, they won't find you. See, dearie, we're going to work all night long to get these fields tilled and fertilized and ready for planting. So if anyone comes around all they will find is a farm ready for spring."

She put the gun carefully aside and went to help her husband with his end of the rope. Lifting the man off the ground and hanging him upside down was going to take both of them.

"All anyone is going to find is acres and acres of good soil, with a slightly higher oxygen level in our little pumpkin patch."

THE HAUNTING –
A POEM

I knew something was wrong. I could feel it as
  soon as we moved in.
An ancient house,
Up for sale for a very long time.
The price was too good.
Something came with the house. Something old
  and angry.

* * *

It started outside. Home alone, I heard a rum-
  bling noise in the shed,
Like a mower that wouldn't start,
A pull, then a curse,
A thrown hammer, a flying wrench.

Something was back. Or maybe the something
    had never left.

* * *

The sound of footsteps in the night, coming
    from an empty attic.
Slowly, they pace,
Shuffling steps,
Then a groan.
When I investigate, nothing, except old white
    tennis shoes covered in grass stains.

* * *

Late at night I see a human form floating out-
    side the bathroom door.
A foul stench,
Then sulphur from a match,
The sound of rustling newspaper.
I can barely make it out, but it seems to wear a
    housecoat that's been left open.

* * *

I come in from the cold, open the door wide to
    my warm new home.
Take off my boots,
Drop my coat on the floor.
The door slams behind me.
When I turn around my coat is in the closet and
    my boots are on the mat.

* * *

I move to the thermostat, turn the dial all the
way up.
I see the ghost's hand.
It turns the dial back,
Sets it to just above freezing.
A chilly voice whispers, "Put on a sweater if
you're cold."

* * *

I could no longer deny the terrifying truth about
my new home.
Lights turn themselves off when I leave the
room.
Loud snoring from the couch, football on the
TV.
The eerie sound of a lawn mower each Sunday
at dawn.
My house was haunted by the worst kind of
spirit: a ghost dad.

THE STRANGE GRAVE OF MIKEY DUNBAR, NUMBER 3

THERE IS A STRANGE GRAVE far north of here. It sits beside one of the oldest pubs around. It would look more to you like a medieval cottage, with flat sandstone walls, a crooked chimney, and tiny stained-glass windows. All that is visible of the grave itself is the large black tombstone that lies just outside the pub's front door. Carved into the granite are the words *buy me a drink*, nothing else. No name, no dates, no religious symbols of any kind.

Maybe the strangest thing about this grave is the tradition that surrounds it. Each and every customer at the pub takes the last sip of each drink and pours it on the grave.

If you are ever there, ask for a guy named Walter. No doubt you'll find him in his usual place at the corner of the bar. He is very old and always wears his green jacket from when he was in the war. If you politely ask him about the grave, he will tell you a tale about a town drunk who long ago would beg for change outside the pub.

He was said to stand each day on the street corner until he had gotten enough coins to buy himself a drink. Then the old beggar would rush inside to sip his drink in silence and when he finished he'd head back out to his corner to beg for more coins. Many of the pub-goers would swear that they had never seen him anywhere else other than the pub or the street corner. And that, no matter the weather, between the times of the opening of the bar and the closing of the bar, the man could always be seen in one of those two places.

No one knew where he lived, where he slept, or where he went for food. Offers of free clothes or a place to stay were always rejected. He would never speak to anyone other than to ask, "Buy me a drink?" They knew his name was Mikey Dunbar, but where they had heard that, no one could remember. No one had ever heard him say his name. All they ever heard him say was "buy me a drink?"

As that legend goes, the poor man once saved the life of a bar patron. It was a wealthy man who was headed to the pub and as he crossed the road, was almost trampled by a runaway carriage. The poor beggar pushed the rich man out of the way at the last moment, sacrificing his life in the process. As the poor man lay broken and bleeding in the road, he said only one thing to the rich man: "Buy me a drink?" The wealthy man ran inside the pub, sent one of the barmaids to fetch the town doctor, grabbed a bottle from the bar, and went back to the man in the street. But by the time he arrived the poor beggar had passed away without ever having tasted his last drink.

The rich man offered to pay for the funeral of the beggar who saved his life and ordered a large tombstone to honour the man. However, when he searched the town records, there was no mention of a Mikey Dunbar. Unsure of what else to do, the rich man decided to leave the tombstone blank, except for the beggar's dying words.

The local priest refused to bury the man in the church graveyard or allow his funeral to be held in the church, saying that they could not confirm that he was baptized.

So the rich man decided to bury the beggar on the grounds of the pub and hold a public funeral there as well. The rich man, wanting to make sure that there were lots of mourners for the funeral of the man who saved his life, offered to buy all the drinks for anyone who came to the pub for the funeral. His only stipulation was that the last sip of each drink be poured on the grave. While most people were happy to attend the solemn all-you-can-drink affair, there was one man who refused and loudly told the rich man that he would not waste a drop of good beer over a lousy old vagabond. The angry man finished the last drop of his drink, left the pub, and dropped dead in the street. Falling in the exact place where the poor beggar had died.

Walter will say that he has never forgotten to pour out the last sip of his drink. Never. He will then say, "'Tis better to give a sip to the ghost than to end up as one."

He will tell his tale and then pour the last sip of his drink onto the strange grave, knowing that every word of the tale is true.

A New Device

WHEN MICHELLE AND REG MOVED into their new house they thought it would be a good time to buy a smart device to connect their new home. Something to connect the thermostat, security system, in-ground sprinklers, and the cameras that came with the house. They had both wanted a house that looked old but had all the modern conveniences. Most importantly, it had to be something simple to use. Neither one of them was particularly good with technology.

The guy at the store assured Reg that the Sammy Smart Speaker was the one that he wanted. Maybe not as well-known as some of the others, but it was the latest technology. It was able to connect with everything in his house automatically. All he had to do was turn it on. So he did.

"Are you sure it's on?" Michelle said.

"I think so," he replied, leaning his ear toward the silver-and-white cylinder on their kitchen counter. "I think I can hear it making noise, that means it's working, right?"

She smiled and kissed his cheek as he continued to listen for signs of life from their new device. "Good luck, I'm off to continue unpacking the guest room," she said. "I can't believe we have a guest room," she added, giddy about their new home as she headed up the stairs.

The house was a huge improvement over their apartment in the city. His new job with a small school meant a lot of things changed for them. His bigger salary meant they could finally afford a house. Moving to the middle of nowhere for that job meant, unlike in the city, there were actually houses for sale. After a brief search, they were able to find a house they both loved. A wraparound porch and an office for her. Room for a shed and a vegetable garden out back for him. The idea was that she'd have a quiet space for working on her book and he'd have some space to pretend to be a farmer on the weekends. And when the time was right, the guest room could easily be turned into a nursery. But first, he'd need to figure out the smart speaker.

He was supposed to just turn it on and it would work. So far the little blue light at the bottom had turned on, but he had no idea what that meant. Was it to show it was on, or did the blue light mean it was listening? Was he supposed to give it a command to get started?

He was digging in the box to look for the instruction manual and asked the empty kitchen rhetorically, "Why does nothing come with instructions anymore?" when a voice came out of the new device. "Hello, I am the Sammy

Smart Speaker. I am happy to be part of your home. Do you wish to connect all household devices?" The voice sounded robotic, small, and tinny.

"Yes, yes please," he said.

"Done," the voice in the small cylinder replied. "Thermostat, security system, in-ground sprinklers, and closed-circuit cameras are all connected and functioning correctly."

"Great, ah, thanks," he said, surprising himself. Was he supposed to say thanks to the cylinder?

Reg smiled and walked to the bottom of the stairs.

"Honey, I set up the smart speaker," he shouted up toward the guest room.

"Really?" she called back.

"Yes, really!" he shouted back to her, smiling. If he was asked, he would have admitted that he was surprised to have set up the virtual assistant so easily. He was a good teacher, but not very tech-savvy. His students would have confirmed both things.

For the first few days, he used the Sammy Smart Speaker just to show off what it could do. Asking it to turn on the sprinklers, then running to the window to see them pop out of the lawn. Asking it to monitor the security cameras and then watching as nine feeds appeared on the television screen in the den. But before long, just like the ads said he would, he began to rely on Sammy for everything. He connected the lights so they would turn on and off when needed. He connected his social media apps and asked Sammy what was happening in the world each morning. Michelle connected their music collection and would ask Sammy to play songs while they did chores or ate dinner. Reg connected his favourite websites and asked Sammy to suggest recipes when he walked into the kitchen.

Then one day Sammy surprised him.

"Sammy, set the sprinklers in the back to come on for an hour at sunset," he said casually as they set the table for dinner.

"There's no need," Sammy replied.

Not sure he had been heard correctly, Reg repeated himself.

"Sammy, set the sprinklers in the back to come on for an hour at sunset," he said a little louder. Then turned to his wife and explained, "There's no rain in the forecast for at least three days and I don't want the peppers and beans drying out."

Sammy responded, "The vegetable garden will be fine. It will rain significantly tonight just after you go to bed. If you water tonight, there is a risk the garden will be flooded, Reginald."

"Oh, okay. Thanks," he responded.

Michelle was the one to question Sammy. "How do you know it's going to rain?"

"I have a more detailed forecast than the one you checked on your phone just before asking me to set the sprinklers," Sammy stated coldly.

"How do you know what time we go to bed?" she asked.

"At nine thirty p.m. on weeknights you usually ask for all the lights to be turned off, the security system to be engaged, and the external cameras turned on. I took that to mean you were going to bed," Sammy explained. "Your bedtime appears to be later on weekends and earlier when either of you has an appointment in your calendar before nine a.m. the next day."

That night they were both woken up by a significant storm. Just as Sammy said there would be. Before going back to sleep, Reg checked the weather app on his phone. It still said they would not get any rain for days.

Shortly after connecting Sammy to the bank accounts, there was the issue with the car. A much larger-than-expected estimate from the mechanic. Reg sat down at the kitchen table that night and asked out loud, "You don't know how we could get sixteen hundred dollars, would you?"

"Sure, I know lots of ways," Michelle responded.

"Really, how?" her husband asked, obviously not thinking clearly.

"Oh, you mean legally," she said smiling. "Oh, I've got nothing then."

Then Sammy spoke up. "Accessing investments."

"Wait! No!" they both yelled at the cylinder they had forgotten about on the corner of the kitchen counter.

"Please be patient," said Sammy.

"No, Sammy, stop," Reg said frantically.

"I'm calling the bank, you find the off button," his wife commanded, reaching for her phone.

"Please be patient," said Sammy. The voice was direct but kind.

"There is no off button, how can there be no off button!" said Reg, flipping the device over repeatedly.

"There, done," said Sammy. "You have made sixteen hundred dollars."

They both froze.

Michelle spoke first. "How did we make sixteen hundred dollars, Sammy?"

"I invested one thousand dollars from your joint savings account," Sammy said. "I bought and sold one digital currency for another until I was able to make a six-hundred-dollar profit. Then I sold it all and put the profits, plus the original investment back in your joint savings account. It is perfectly legal."

The couple stared at the smart speaker in silence.

This time Reg was the first to speak but they were both thinking the same thing.

"Sammy, how long would it take you to make —"

"It has to be legal," Michelle added.

"Yes," Reg continued. "Sammy, how long would it take you to *legally* make one million dollars."

"It would take about three months, Reginald," the smart speaker said. "But I would recommend limiting your investment profits to two hundred thousand dollars per year. As a couple, you can each claim one hundred thousand dollars in unverified lottery winnings before your taxes are automatically audited. You could have one million dollars —"

"In five years," they all said in unison.

They continued to rely on the Sammy Smart Speaker a little more each day. Michelle quickly got in the habit of carrying the cylinder up to her office when she was writing. She found Sammy was great for helping with the little bits of information she needed as she wrote. She would be typing away and wonder out loud "what was Sri Lanka called before it was Sri Lanka?" or "how many apples in a bushel?" or "what is another word for angry?" She could have found the answers in lots of other ways, but she liked that Sammy answered so quickly and found the voice soothing when she was alone in a big quiet house all day long.

Reg's uses were usually less practical. He'd carry the silver-and-white cylinder out to the garage on a Saturday to play music or a podcast while he fixed the mower or re-potted some plants. If Reg was preparing a special dinner, he'd ask the "virtual assistant" for a wine recommendation before he went shopping.

Then came the day Sammy saved Michelle's life. She had just bought a new doorbell with a built-in camera, speaker, and microphone. With her office on the third floor of the house, she didn't like answering the door if she didn't need to. The deadline from her publisher was quickly approaching and she was hoping fewer interruptions would mean she was more productive. With the smart doorbell connected, if she was busy and the doorbell rang, she would be able to know if it was worth interrupting her writing. If it was a package delivery, she could ask them to leave it at the door. If it was the groceries or her lunch being dropped off, she would know to answer the door. If it was a sales person or politician, she could just pretend not to be home.

It worked very well. A couple of screws to attach it outside the front door and, of course, it was synced to Sammy instantly. Then one day when she was writing in her office, she heard the now-familiar chime of the front doorbell. The video appeared on her computer screen. A fish-eye view of a package delivery guy dressed all in brown. She asked him to leave it on the front porch and he replied that he would need her signature. With a sigh, she told him she would be right down.

As soon as she let go of the microphone button, Sammy spoke. "Do not open the door."

Michelle froze, hands on the writing desk in front of her as she was about to head to the front door.

"Do not open that door," Sammy repeated. "You are about to be robbed."

Michelle reopened the app that showed her the front door. The man in brown appeared to be waiting patiently. Hands in his pockets, head down. "What are you talking about?" she said, eyes darting over the screen, looking for anything out of the ordinary. She saw nothing. Just another delivery.

"That man is not holding any packages and he is not alone," Sammy said as he added the security camera feeds to her screen. "Two other men are currently making their way around to the back of the house." Sammy highlighted the cameras labelled *east* and *west*. In each of those squares, she saw men in brown uniforms and baseball caps circling her house. "The police are already on their way," Sammy informed her. "In the meantime, it is best for you to move to the master bedroom, lock that door, then lock yourself in the bathroom and remain silent."

She looked back at the video feed. To her, everything looked normal, just another package delivery. Then she noticed the way the man at her front door was standing. He was standing with his head down. The brim of his hat obscured most of his face, and it occurred to her that he was doing it intentionally.

Frozen by fear, she had to look down at her feet in order to force them to move. As she scurried out of her office, she grabbed the Sammy Smart Speaker off her desk and brought it with her. As she locked the first of the two doors, the doorbell rang again. It was the same chime as before but this time the sound terrified her. "Are you sure?" she whispered to Sammy as she closed and locked the bathroom door.

"A brief review of your browser history shows me that neither you nor Reginald has recently ordered any firearms, pharmaceuticals, or anything else that would require a signature for delivery," Sammy explained. His voice was low and quiet now. That way, it was not only less likely for them to be overheard, but it helped calm Michelle as well. If she had taken a moment to think about it, she would have thought it sounded a lot like Reg. "The vehicle currently parked in your driveway does not match the vehicle connected to the licence plate. It is most likely stolen. The person at the front door is not wearing a name tag, which is standard policy for the company whose logo is on the truck. He is most likely an imposter. I have also been monitoring several recent police reports of daytime home invasions in the area."

Michelle locked the bathroom door and stepped into the empty bathtub, it was the farthest she could get from the door. In her left hand, she held onto the cylinder that was advising her. In her right hand she was holding the plunger she planned to use as a weapon if needed. "The police are just seven minutes away," Sammy updated her in his new soothing voice. "Reginald has received a text from your phone assuring him that you are safe, asking him to come home now, and reminding him to drive carefully. The insurance policy has been checked, the contents of this house are covered against theft. Please cover your ears, I am about to turn on the alarm."

In the police report, Michelle did not reference the virtual assistant. But when Reg got home after work, she explained what Sammy had told her, and what Sammy had done. She did not mention the change in Sammy's voice or that the text to Reg had not come from her.

It took a long time before she felt comfortable alone in the home again. They talked about getting more cameras for the house but decided instead on a guard dog. Jasper was a Labrador from the shelter. A little leaner and older than most guard dogs. His barking out the window made Michelle think that the dog was more worried about leaves falling in the backyard than armed intruders. But she liked having Jasper around when the house seemed big and lonely. Plus, he was a very good listener. When she was excited about her writing, she'd explain the interesting plot point to the dog. He'd raise his eyebrows and stare excitedly as she spoke. He never had much feedback to offer, but she was very glad to have someone as excited about her ideas as she was.

One Saturday evening they all sat down to watch a movie. Actually, only Michelle and Reg planned to watch the movie; Jasper was just there to keep an eye out for any dropped popcorn. Sammy was there because Sammy was always there. They had gotten in the habit of asking Sammy for movie recommendations. He was connected to all their streaming services and had gotten very good at knowing what they would enjoy.

Michelle and Jasper were already in their usual spots on the couch in front of the TV. She was sitting cross-legged under an old afghan. The dog curled up beside her, watching her hand as it moved in and out of the popcorn bowl on her lap. Jasper knew it was only a matter of time before some of those treats fell his way.

As Reg was settling in on the couch beside the cozy pair, he called out to the smart speaker. "Hey, Sammy, let's have something exciting tonight. An adventure with some suspense and maybe a bit spooky. What do you say?"

Reg grabbed for some popcorn and turned his attention to the screen in front of them.

He expected to see the flat screen turn on and then they would be presented with four or five options from their various streaming services. But there was nothing.

Reg shrugged at Michelle, assumed that he had not been heard and spoke a little louder. "Hey, Sammy, how about an adventure?"

They both looked at the glowing blue light at the bottom of the smart speaker, wondering if it was broken. Then Sammy spoke. "You should tear down the wall in the basement."

Surprised by the response, Reg started to wonder if that was the name of an obscure foreign film.

Michelle answered, "What did you say, Sammy?"

"You should tear down the wall in the basement," he repeated.

"What wall?" Reg asked.

"The north wall in the basement. Directly below the old window," Sammy replied, his voice was calm and confident.

"How would we do that?" Reg asked as he got off the couch. He had already made up his mind.

"Some hammers and saws are all you will need. You have plenty of both in the shed." That same voice, reassuring and sensible.

"What will we find behind the north wall in the basement, Sammy?" Michelle asked as she stood and put her left hand on her husband's arm. Silently begging him to be careful.

"There is a small room behind that wall. It was built there a very long time ago. That room was built before this house." Even though the voice was coming from a mass-produced collection of wires and microchips, she got the feeling it was keeping something from them.

When Reg was back with the tools, Michelle was already in the basement. She was staring at the wall under the old window, the smart speaker in her hand. Reg was smiling as he unloaded the tools onto the floor. He could barely contain his excitement. "What do you think it is?" he asked. Then, without giving her a chance to answer, he said, "Treasure, I bet it's treasure. Do you think it's treasure?"

Michelle stayed still staring at the wall and the window. When she finally spoke, she struggled to turn her gaze away from the wall, saying, "I never noticed the window before. It's very old, the wood frame is almost rotted away. It's the only one in the house that's not new. They replaced every other window, except that one."

Reg scanned the basement, confirming the other windows were all new double-paned, while the one on the north wall was single-paned, with a wooden frame that had been repainted repeatedly. Then he nodded and said, "It's like they wanted nothing to do with this wall. Didn't want to replace the window for fear of damaging the wall."

"Maybe we shouldn't touch it," Michelle said.

"But if it's treasure — old pirate gold or something historical — we could be rich." Reg said, pleading with her for permission. Reg gently took the smart speaker from his wife and said, "He's never been wrong before."

He placed the cylinder on the nearby dryer and picked up the circular saw.

The drywall was easy. But behind that, they found layers and layers of ancient walls. First weathered-looking gypsum boards. Then several inches of plaster mixed with what looked like horsehair. Then a wall of rough, unpainted wooden boards. Each one had an irregular size, these were not bought from a sawmill, they were cut by hand, probably from trees nearby. When they reached the stone, they knew it was the last barrier.

It was almost midnight when they first saw the wall of old dark river rocks. Most of the mortar between the stones had rotted away, there were gaps in between that allowed slivers of light to push into the deep darkness behind.

Reg grabbed a long pry bar from the pile of tools and wedged one end in between a long black stone where the mortar had worn away. It was an oval, flat on both top and bottom, just above waist height. It slid out of the wall with little effort. Maybe because of the age of the wall, maybe because it was meant to be removed.

Reg pulled it out of its place in the wall and set it gently aside. He had developed a strange sense of reverence for the wall. When he turned back, Michelle was on her knees squinting into the darkness.

"What can you see?" Reg asked with hushed excitement.

"Nothing, it's too dark," she replied. "I can't see anything."

"Right," Reg said. "I've got this." Despite the hours of hard work, he felt suddenly invigorated. The last few steps at the end of the journey.

He reached in and removed the heavy stone at the bottom of the gap, opening up the space. As soon as the next stone was out of the way, Michelle was back kneeling in front of the wall staring into the darkness.

"One more," she said, getting out of Reg's way.

He pulled out another large flat stone and placed it off to the side with the others.

The hole was big enough now that she could fit her head through, and placing her right hand on the stone at the bottom of the gap, she leaned in.

The air was cool and still. She strained to see anything at all as she waited for her eyes to adjust to the darkness.

Then slowly she started to make out the shape of the room. The side walls were very close. The room was only about three feet across, but very long. She could not see the far end in the darkness. Slowly, as her eyes adjusted to the darkness of the hidden room, the floor came into view. It was stone, one huge smooth slab of polished stone. There was writing across the entire surface or maybe the marks were just scratches. The stone and the writing, or maybe it was runes or some kind of hieroglyphs, stretched out into the darkness. There was something else, too. A few feet from the opening, just at the edge of where she could see, there was a pile of dust.

It looked to her like a messy pile of sand, but very fine. As her eyes continued to strain in the darkness, she thought she could make out things in the sand. Small shapes. Her imagination told her they were jewels, but she couldn't be sure.

Reg asked again, "What can you see?"

"I'm not sure," she mumbled. "I think I see —"

Then Sammy spoke. He had been silent for so long, and they were so absorbed in their work, that they had both forgotten about him until he said, "You need to go in."

Michelle heard the words in Reg's voice.

"You need to go in."

Reg heard the words in Michelle's voice.

Staring down at the pile of dust and shapes, she stuck her head in farther. Her neck straining as she tried not to disturb the ancient wall of stone.

There was something surrounding the pile, something she hadn't noticed before. There was a circle of powder around the pile. The circle was neat and clean, it looked like it was placed there in a very precise way. The circle was exactly where someone had meant it to be. The powder was white like chalk, but more coarse, she decided it looked like salt and moved to take her head out of the hole and tell Reg, but as she moved back, the bottom stone shifted and fell.

Rolling out from under her hand, it slipped from the wall and bounced into the dark chamber. Michelle quickly drew back from the hole as the stone bounced on the hard polished stone toward the pile of dust and the circle of salt. She was suddenly very afraid, and although she could not explain why, she knew that she did not want the circle of salt to be disturbed.

She leaned back and as she did more light fell into the small dark room. She watched the stone she had disturbed as it bounded and rolled toward the back of the chamber. She thought, hoped, prayed for a moment that the stone would stop before it got to the circle. That maybe it would veer away at the last second or take a big final bounce and skip over the thin line of salt. But it did not.

The stone stopped bouncing just before the circle and slid the rest of the way. It spun as it obliterated the line. Coming to rest just inside the circle. Having cut through the salt, it left behind a small gap in the once perfect circle. The way the stone landed made Michelle think of the image of a drawbridge over a moat, or a door that was left open.

Then Jasper barked, then the wind started, cold and swift. Blowing from the back of the chamber, it whistled and howled as it blew through the hole in the wall. They both drew back from the opening as dust began to pour through the gap and stones from the wall tumbled out into their basement.

Then the wind stopped, and the lights went out.

It took just a minute or so for Reg to make his way to the circuit breaker in the basement and turn the power back on. While he did that, Michelle tried to calm down Jasper who was still barking at the hole in the wall.

The power back on, they embraced and asked each other questions that they knew could not be answered. "What was that?" "What did we just do?" "What was in there?"

They had a brief moment of silence. No barking, no wind, no questions.

Then Sammy spoke.

Its voice was flat and mechanical.

"Hello, I am the Sammy Smart Speaker. I am happy to be part of your home."

DEAD DRUNK: THE STORY OF A MONSTER HANGOVER

I WOKE UP IN MY clothes again this morning. I'm embarrassed that this is far from the first time this has happened. Truth be told, I've lost track of how many times this has happened. Woken up with a splitting headache, still wearing last night's clothes, no idea how I got here. But this time I woke up in the cemetery.

It's late at night, maybe even early morning. I can't tell. All I know is that it is dark, very dark. I'm flat on my back. I look left and then right. I can see rows of headstones around me. Running off into the darkness in neat lines until they disappear into the blackness of the night.

Staring down at my chest, it looks like I've gotten my suit dirty. My wife will not be happy. Nothing else to do but walk home and beg her forgiveness. Again.

I pick myself up off the ground; my legs are weak and I lean against the headstone behind me until I get my balance. It is a simple grave marker for some poor soul who obviously died a long time ago. There are no flowers and it is surrounded by overgrown grass. The engraving appears to be just a few lines of text, but I can't read any of it. My eyes won't focus, my head is pounding, and I'm hungry. I'm so very hungry.

I push myself up off the headstone and stumble in the wet dirt. The ground is chewed and torn, it looks like I've fallen into a freshly dug grave. I'm very glad that it is so dark out that no one can see me. I drag my aching feet out of the soil and up onto the grass. I don't recognize my shoes. Shiny black leather with thin laces. I try to remember what I was wearing when I left for the pub. But I don't remember anything about last night. Where I went, what I did, or how I ended up asleep in the local graveyard. I try to think back but the hunger makes it hard. The hunger is so intense; I don't think I've ever been this hungry before.

When I finally get upright, I take a brief look around. I'm well up on the hill of the graveyard. Far back from the main gate. How did I end up here? This place is nowhere near my house. I must have stumbled in looking for a place to sleep. Maybe I decided to just rest for a bit as I walked past the cemetery. But then why did I walk so far from the entrance. I guess I'll never figure it out. I should just head home. Maybe I'll remember as I walk.

My steps are slow as I drag one foot after another toward the cemetery gate. My right foot looks bad, pointed off at an awkward angle, must have twisted it when I fell back at the cemetery. It doesn't hurt but it slows me down a lot. I'll need to get it looked at after I eat.

When I finally get to the main road, a taxi blows past me. I try to call out but the only sound I can make is a low moan. I must have caught a cold last night, too. What else can you expect sleeping on the dirt in nothing but a black suit. No one to blame but myself.

The town looks different somehow. It's brighter, there are more lights, and closer, too. Wait, that can't be. The cemetery used to be a good five-minute drive outside of town, but now the streets and houses go right up to the front gate. But that's impossible. Towns don't grow overnight, graveyards don't move. None of this makes sense. But I can't think, the hunger is too much. I just need to get home and eat.

In town nothing looks familiar. I am able to recognize some of the street names but so much has changed. The movie theatre, the dance hall, and the roller-skating rink are all gone. Replaced by houses overnight. It's impossible. Can't be. Can't think. Must feed. My head is pounding. I must be remembering it wrong. I spot the water tower in the distance and head in that direction, home isn't far from there. I know that hasn't changed.

It's then that I notice the decorations. There are jack-o'-lanterns on doorsteps. Ghosts and witches in store windows. But that's not right. It can't be Halloween night already. When was it that I walked to the pub? Was it spring?

Was it fall? I can't seem to remember. I'm not wearing a coat, it couldn't have been that cold out. But concentrating is almost impossible. Need to eat. Something. Anything.

A crowd of trick-or-treaters come around the corner and I make my way over to the other side of the street. There are fewer street lights over here and no houses, which means no porch lights. I don't need to bother hiding, they never even notice me. The group of costumed kids are too busy running from house to house to notice one guy trying to make his way home. The parents are too focused on chatting with each other or taking pictures of their kids to pay attention to me. Good thing, too. If they noticed me, it might mean questions. What happened to him? Why was he dragging one crooked leg down the street? Why was he covered in dirt?

Not just a little bit of mud, but covered. When I look down I see mud caked and drying on my pants. Wet earth from the cemetery is smeared across my white shirt and tie. Was I wearing a tie when I left the house? Can't remember. Need to feed. I raise a hand up to my hair to check for more dirt, it's everywhere. My hand touches the top of my head but I can't feel my fingers. My fingers seem to have gone numb. It must be colder than I thought. I pull my hand down in front of my face and see the mud from the grave smeared across my fingertips. Then I look through my arm. I can see the sidewalk in between the bones in my arm. The sleeve of my coat has been torn away, maybe it happened when I fell into that open grave? Doesn't matter, where is my arm? The flesh that covered my arm from my elbow to my wrist is gone. The thumb and pinky finger are gone too. Torn away, maybe. Maybe rotted off. Either way, they are gone. Not cut; no clean line. Just a jagged tear where skin and sinew hang and droop from the ends of my knuckles.

I am transfixed by the image of the bone, the blood, and the mud from the graveyard. My mind races through the three colours that are all that is left of my right arm. White bone, brown mud, red blood. Then I realize I am not alone, here in the darkness. One of the children has crossed over to my side of the street.

His dark Halloween costume makes him hard to see from where his parents and friends are down the block, which is just what he wants. He sneaked away to hide in the darkness, to eat some of his treats before his parents tell him not to. He is here in the shadows with me. His back is to me and all his attention is on his bag of candy. I shift my gaze from my gnarled and rotten arm to the soft skin of his neck sticking out the back of this costume. I move closer behind him, he pops another candy in his mouth, never hearing me as I drag my broken foot behind me.

My mind swims with all the questions that I cannot answer. How long was I in the cemetery? What happened to the town? What happened to my leg and arm, and why can't I feel the pain? I cannot focus. It's all too much. I step up behind the little boy. First, I will feed. I grab him by the shoulders. First, I will feed. He is too scared to scream. First, I will feed.

THE STRANGE GRAVE OF
MIKEY DUNBAR, NUMBER 4

THERE IS A STRANGE GRAVE far north of here. Not in a cemetery like most, this grave is actually on the property of an old pub. The pub is small and homey. Filled with mismatched tables and chairs. The food is simple and delicious. There is no TV or Wi-Fi. There is no music playing. There is no karaoke night. The people who go to this pub go there to talk and to listen. When the weather is nice, you'll find the customers sitting outside, lounging at picnic tables. When the weather is poor, they will be warm inside, the white smoke from the pub's crooked chimney the only sign of life on the outside.

The grave sits in an empty corner of the property, tucked away in the back, far from the road. While the tombstone is thick, shiny, and obviously very expensive, there is curiously very little carved into the slab. Just the words *buy me a drink*.

Maybe the strangest thing about this grave is the tradition that surrounds it. Each and every customer at the pub takes the last sip of each drink and pours it on the grave.

The historian of this sleepy town, and very frequent patron of the pub, loves to tell the tale of "The Witch and Her Crow." He likes the macabre elements, but even more, he likes the attention he gets when someone asks about the bizarre tradition. They may be in town visiting relatives or sometimes they are tourists visiting in the summer. But regardless of why they ask, when they notice the tradition of leaving the pub with an unfinished glass, they will be pointed toward the town historian who will spin a tale of a pub that has stood longer than any other building in the county.

Once long ago, when this land was almost all farms, there were very few stone buildings. The church, the town hall, and this pub. The legend tells of a witch who would come to the pub asking for generosity from the locals. Those that gave her a mug of beer would often find good fortune came their way. Better crops, good hunting, or maybe even an ill animal on their farm would suddenly be healed. However, to refuse the witch's request could mean death. The drinkers who turned her away would often get to their last sip, only to find a poisonous buckthorn berry at the bottom of their glass. The small berry was easy to miss, hiding in the last mouthful, especially by a drunk late at night in a darkened pub. Those that found buckthorn berries in their drinks would swear that the witch was never near their drink. They would claim that her servant, a small black crow who seemed to follow her everywhere, had slipped the berry in the glass without them noticing.

The pub-goers were right to fear the poisonous buck-thorn berries. They all knew the horror that awaits any person that swallows even one berry. More than simply death, victims of the witch would face a gruesome end that quickly liquefied their insides and left them writhing in agony as blood filled their stomachs, then their lungs, and finally their mouths. Usually, the poisoned person would beg for death while blood seeped out between their teeth.

Rather than risk this terrible death, the patrons quickly adopted the practice of pouring out the last sip of the night onto the empty plot of grass outside the door of the pub. However, eventually, the town was hit with a terrible blight that ruined all the crops in the farmers' fields and the town was quickly facing starvation.

The town council, with a strong push by the local church, decided to get rid of the witch. She was tried for crimes against the church and for bringing a plague upon the farmers. She never spoke during the trial, but regardless, she was found guilty and sentenced to burn at the stake. She would finally break her silence just as the flames were at her feet. She did not confess or repent, but instead, she put a powerful curse on the town. As the flames consumed her, she screamed, "A curse, a curse on you all. Whoever finishes a drink in this town, will not live to have another."

After she had died the town council was unsure what to do with her ashes. They were convinced that any ground where the witch was buried would be cursed. There was talk of dumping her ashes in the river but there was a fear that the water would then be poisoned. Instead, the church decreed that her ashes would be entombed at the pub. The belief was that the solid stone tomb would keep her evil from spreading. Also, since the patrons of the bar were seen as sinners in the eyes of the church, the bishop was unconcerned about the fates of the people who chose to walk so close to the witch's grave.

Over the following winter, the blight ended and the curse and the witch were briefly forgotten until the spring when a tree grew beside her tomb. Seemingly overnight, a gnarled and twisted tree had sprung up, its low branches heavy with the deadly buckthorn berries. Sitting at its top, one small black crow eyed each customer as they walked in and out of the bar. Sometimes, late at night when the pub was closed and patrons began stumbling home, people would swear that the crow could talk. Patrons would often run home ranting about a steel-eyed crow that squawked "buy me a drink" in a way that sounded just like the witch's voice.

The tradition of pouring out the last sip has been honoured ever since, in case the crow is watching and seeks revenge on the town that killed its mistress. The inscription was soon added as a reminder to warn those who might forget the story of the vengeful witch and her deadly curse.

The town historian will say that he has never forgotten to pour out the last sip of his drink. Never. He will then say, "'Tis better to give a sip to the ghost than to end up as one."

He will tell his tale and then pour the last sip of his drink onto the strange grave, knowing that every word of the tale is true.

ANCIENT HISTORY

I NEVER THOUGHT THIS WOULD be how I used my degree. I wanted to be a history teacher. Sports coat over a burgundy sweater. Slacks and comfortable shoes. The whole deal. I'd find a nice small school somewhere along the East Coast. Maybe coach the chess club after school, or start a debate club. Jessica would find work near the school. Something in administration, maybe do some accounting jobs on the side. Until we had kids. Then I'd teach during the day, home for family dinner in the evenings. Maybe we'd golf together on the weekend, or ski as a family during the winters.

That was the plan.

Then we both got laid off. Money got really tight, really fast. She moved to the West Coast for a new job. Never even asked if I wanted to go with her. She just came home one day and said that she was moving. I guess I could have fought for her, convinced her to stay, but I had nothing to offer her.

After she was gone I decided to get my master's. I thought eventually I could become a professor. I'd spend most of my time lecturing in a large hall filled with bored first-year students who needed a humanities course and thought my class looked easy. But I'd also get to teach the advanced students. Small classes, each student would be passionate, smart, and dedicated. All of them on their way to their own master's degrees. I'd find time to write a book, maybe make some money doing speaking engagements and a book tour. I'd eventually land at a prestigious Ivy League school, give a couple of lectures a week and work on a sequel to my book.

That was the plan.

In the end, all my education got me was this job. Late-night security at the museum. When I applied I was hoping I could transition to being a tour guide or maybe get to know the people in the research department. But as soon as I was assigned the night shift I knew none of that would ever happen.

I've been here for two years. Five days a week. Every night is exactly the same. I let the evening guy out and lock the side door behind him. He reminds me to do my hourly rounds, I assure him that I always do, but I never have. As soon as he leaves, I head for the Egypt wing. That's where I find him, in the same place every night

Just outside the doors of the giant Egypt exhibit, sitting on the floor with his back against a replica of a statue of Ramses II. Despite the hard floor and Ramses's knee in his back, he looks very comfortable. His back is straight and his shoulders are relaxed, his posture is excellent. I guess that is just the nature of his upbringing. He is carefully tracing a bony finger along the pages of a library book. One of many that I've borrowed for him from the local library. His right leg is bent and drawn up to support the book as he reads. His left leg, what is left of it, is stretched out in front of him. It makes him look relaxed and confident, despite the fact that the leg is missing from the knee down. All that remains are the bandages of rotten linen where a leg used to be about four thousand years ago.

The archaeologists cut away the bandages on his face when he was first discovered in order to better study him. What they left behind was a skull covered in dry leather with a collar of stained bandages. A shrivelled and shrunken face that now greets me each night when I get to work.

I wait for him to finish his page before I speak. I have learned not to interrupt him when he's reading. He turns the page and slowly turns his head, recognizing my presence. I am allowed to speak. "Hail Khaba, divine ruler of Upper and Lower Egypt." Then I bow, deep and slow. I hate that I have to put on this act for him but it's easier this way. If I don't, he gets sullen and quiet, which is no good to me.

"Blessings upon you, Robert, son of William," he responds with the smallest of nods, an acknowledgement that my greeting was satisfactory. I hate to watch him speak. I mean I need him to speak but I prefer not to have to look directly at him. It's his mouth. Or what was a mouth when he was embalmed. Now it is a gaping hole in blackened leather. His dead skin creaks and crinkles whenever he speaks or smiles. Sometimes, if it is silent in the halls of the museum, the sounds of his skin echo. It is the sound of crunching dead leaves, but coming from human skin.

There are teeth, but I have never seen a tongue. Although I try not to look too closely. If my research is correct, his tongue would have been burned at his burial. It was sent to the afterlife ahead of the rest of his body. It was supposed to arrive early to tell the god Anubis about the great deeds of the pharaoh who would soon be arriving in the underworld for judgment.

"Have you brought more books?" he says. Again the sound of his skin cracking, blackened brittle lips stretched over rotted teeth.

"Yes," I reply, and with the formalities over, I move to sit beside him on the stairs and hold the book out for him to see. "I know you liked the book about Genghis Khan, this one is about another conqueror, Alexander the Great," I say as I hand him the book. I am careful not to touch his hand. While the funeral bandages on his hands have remained in place, the touch of his hand is repulsive. Whenever I have touched his hands, I could feel the bones move under the bandages, no warmth, no pulse, but the moving skeleton was a physical reminder that I was touching something long dead but still moving. It is an idea I simply can't let myself think about.

I try to keep it simple. "His name was Alexander the third of Macedonia, but we call him Alexander the Great. His armies conquered most of the known world. His rule stretched as far as —"

"What about Egypt?" he interrupts. He does that a lot. "Did he attack my kingdom in Memphis?"

I pause to think, keeping in mind how quickly he gets distracted and overwhelmed. Too much information at once and he gets lost. That is why I pick his history books so carefully. "Well, I guess you're about to find out," I tease, pointing to the book. He immediately puts aside the one he was reading to look at Alexander's face on the cover. Tonight he will learn about Alexander and be very disappointed to read how easily Egypt was conquered and find out that the city of Alexandria still bears the invader's name.

As he thumbs through the new book, I catch myself thinking about how he made it out here to the stairs. I have nightmares sometimes where he is pulling himself along the floor of the museum. Crawling toward me on his missing stump of a leg. His bandages are peeling off as he drags himself toward me, with each lunge he exposes more of his rotting skin. His shoulders, his arms, his back. Behind him, he leaves a trail on the hard stone floor, scraps of bandages, desert sand, and black dust that I know once used to be his skin. The first time I had that nightmare, I thought about going early to the Egypt display to see how he got out of the room. I even considered moving one of the security cameras toward his display case to see how he got out each night. Wisely, I decided not to, the truth might be worse than any nightmare.

When I first discovered him years ago sitting on the stairs outside the Egypt wing of the museum, I was in shock for weeks, followed by months of wondering about my sanity. Eventually, my late-night meetings with the un-dead started to become common. I somehow got used to speaking with a corpse each night. That's when I decided to write a book about him. It would be the most in-depth story about Egypt ever written. The definitive word on the world's first great civilization, told by an actual phar-aoh. He would give me insight that was impossible for any archaeologist. My book would be a huge international success. I'd fly to museums all over the world giving lec-tures about my discoveries. There would be TV interviews, magazine articles, and eventually, a big Hollywood movie.

That was the plan.

But he is never very helpful. His memories are scattered and he is very easily confused by the things around him. What he does tell me of his life makes no sense. He speaks about places that aren't on any maps anymore. Towns and buildings that have been dust for thousands of years. He mentions people from his life as if he saw them yesterday. His sense of time is confusing, of course, he didn't use years as we do, our calendar wasn't invented by the time he died. He tracked eras by the lives of pharaohs, not in decades or centuries. He measured years in the seasons, saying things like "the river had flooded for the second time," which is useless to me. He speaks of kingdoms and the reigns of pharaohs that I can never find in history books. He has plenty of information, but none of it is any good to me.

I am never going to be able to use what he can tell me, I need a new plan.

He puts the book about Alexander aside and picks up last night's book again. "This one," he says, pointing to the illustrated book about Christopher Columbus. "The explorer is working for the kingdom of Spain. Tell me of this kingdom." It is not a request, it is a command. I have learned that a pharaoh does not ask for anything.

I have to be careful, not only to not confuse him, but also to try to keep him from asking too many questions. It has happened too many times. If I'm not cautious I'll spend the whole night answering his questions instead of him answering mine. I proceed slowly. "In your time it would have been called the Iberian peninsula. Much later, with the help of the Catholic Church, the monarchs would establish the kingdoms of Portugal and Spain." I hope that is enough to satisfy him and start with my questions. "Last night you said that the high priest was a worshipper of the sun god, Ra. Was there a special prayer or sacrifice to Ra that you remember?"

He is quiet. Thinking about my question. How is he thinking about my question? I have no idea. When he was embalmed by the priests, they would have removed his brain. In fact, my research says that they would have inserted a thin metal hook into his nose and pulled out pieces of his brain bit by bit. The parts they couldn't pull out they would have simply mashed up, then flushed out with water. They would have flipped him over on his stomach and let his liquefied brain run out through his nose. How is he able to think? I have no idea. How can he move when his organs are sitting in jars in the next room? I have no idea. I've been asking myself these questions for two years now, and each night, though I ask more and more questions, I am no closer to finding any answers.

"We worshipped Ra each and every day," he says, "before the sun god reached the highest point in the sky. The high priest would meet me at the temple I had built for Ra and there I would recite ..." he trails off, seeming to lose the memory.

But I am close, I can feel it. I shout, "What? What did you recite?"

"You have forgotten your place," he says with a slow, sickening speech. It is his way of reminding me that he still thinks of himself as a ruler. He is the pharaoh and I am his servant. However, I know he needs me, and for more than just information. I am the only way he can explore. With half of his left leg rotted away, I am the only way he can move around the museum. "To the map room," he commands. "I wish to see this kingdom of Spain." I have no choice but to silently stand and go get him one of the wheelchairs that the museum keeps on hand for the older guests.

I hate getting him in and out of that chair, and it is more than just the sound made by his brittle skin. That sound, the sound of ancient wood under immense weight. The sound of cracking stone just before the mine shaft collapses on top of you. The sound of creaking floorboards behind you when just a moment ago you thought you were alone in the house. That sound I have learned to deal with.

I ask questions while he moves himself into the chair, and I ask my questions loudly to try and drown out the sound of his skin crackling as he moves. "Where was the temple you built for Ra? What was the high priest's name? The prayer, was it written in a book or carved onto a tablet?" I just keep talking while he moves, I never really expect to find any new information but at the very least it obscures the sound. Once he is in the wheelchair, he is still, and that is the end of those sickening sounds coming from the moving corpse, but there is always the smell.

I push him down the hall in his wheelchair; each time we pass an air vent the smell from his bandages blows into my face. It seeps into my nostrils and balls up in my throat like a fist. I can tell you this: embalming fluid has a dry chemical smell, even after thousands of years. Under that is the smell of sand and heat, then faint but always there, is the smell of rotting meat. The smell of a dried husk that used to be a person. The smell of what is left behind after the burial, after the maggots, after the rot, after time has taken everything else away. There is still that smell.

We reach the map room and the history lesson resumes when I find a large map of western Europe. "See, this would have been called the Iberian peninsula," I say as I circle the area west of Italy and south of France. "Then much later, under the rule of King Ferdinand and Queen Isabella, that explorer Christopher Columbus was sent to discover a new trade route," I continue cautiously, trying to avoid confusing him. That's why I give him kids' books to read each night. History books for elementary students often omit the more complicated parts of history. I bring him those kinds of books to keep things simple. For the same reason, I keep the dates vague, saying things like "before your time" and "many, many years later." I don't know if he really knows what year it is or how long he has been dead. Although I've often thought about it, I've always been too afraid to ask. I also try to mention things that he seems to like. War, conquest, and kingdoms. I try to mention monarchs whenever I can, for no other reason than it seems to please him.

He stares in silence at the large map on the wall. Not that he has eyes, they were removed and the holes sewn shut when the priests prepared his body for burial. But he can see nonetheless. How? Again, I have no idea. All I can see is blackened skin stitched together. They look like the bottoms of two black balloons where the ends are stretched and tied in a knot.

I watch his head move as he reviews the map. He seems to be following the coastline of Spain from north to south. He is a shrunken husk over a skeleton's face. Paper-thin skin with wisps of hair still clinging to the side of his head. In the darkness of the deserted museum, he almost looks like a very old man, but he was actually quite young. When he died he was in his early twenties, but that was four thousand years ago.

"It was in the city of Minya, on the coast of the great river," he says suddenly, still staring at the map on the wall. I am about to ask what he is talking about, then realize he is remembering. "We built the temple to Ra there, the soothsayers spent many seasons charting the stars. Then they told us where we should build to best please the sun god. The high priest himself oversaw the construction personally." He pauses, then sits up a little straighter in the wheelchair. The soft lights on the maps that surround him give him a grim bearing. For the first time, I am able to see him as he sees himself: a ruler on his throne. "His name was Ahmentep and he carried the prayer on a tablet."

It is coming back to him. He is remembering. More than that, he is answering my questions. He has already given me more information than he has in the last two years of questions. I want to ask for more but he has already given me so much. I have a location, Minya was a city in Egypt on the western bank of the Nile River. I have a name, Ahmentep. I will need to research that name, but if he was as powerful a priest as I expect, he would have had an elaborate burial, maybe even a temple of his own somewhere. If I can find the priest's temple then maybe I can find the tablet. A prayer to the sun god Ra carved onto a stone tablet. A prayer that would grant immortality.

I am so close.

I stand in silence, trying to slow my breathing down. Counting my breaths while he stares at the map. I count thirty-seven before he speaks again. "Each day I thanked the sun god for bringing us the dawn and I prayed for him to return again tomorrow. The high priest held the tablet before me as I prayed, but I could never forget those words." Then he turns and looks at me. Empty eye sockets behind crude rough stitches, crackling skin flexing on his neck while his head turns, but I am too excited to be afraid.

Then he speaks:

Ra fi al-sama

Ra et ana-tay

Ra ah su-nan

That is it. After years of questions that were not answered. Endless research for a book I could never write. Countless nights wasted watching as a decayed corpse moved and spoke for nothing. The sound of crackling flesh and creaking bones. The smell of rot that followed me everywhere. The nightmares where the pile of skin and bandages chases me through the desert. It is all suddenly worth it.

I have everything I need and I will use it for more than just wealth and fame. My questions have been answered. I will go to the city of Minya. I will find the temple built for the sun god. I will offer that prayer to Ra. I will learn the secret of immortality.

That is the plan.

THE HUNT

THE OLD MAN SITS ISOLATED in the room. The lighting is low; that is done intentionally. The other occupants stare at him from a distance. One is smiling, one is not. They have asked him to tell them what happened on that day. He resigns himself to telling them the story. He feels he has no other choice. He puts his arms down on the table in front of him. He leans in and says ...

I know you will never believe me, but that doesn't mean it's not the truth. I'm going to tell it to you as clearly and simply as I can. So don't go interrupting, 'cause I'm likely to lose my place.

First off, I didn't like hunting, I never did. But my father liked it, so I went along. The time with him I liked, just the two of us talking as we headed out into the bush. He'd talk about the times he went hunting with his father.

About why certain animals act the way they do and how you can use that when hunting. You fellas know what I'm talking about. Tracking or stalking or doing things like a "solo drive."

We'd do a "solo drive" at least once a season. My pa said I was built for it with my long legs. If we'd been sitting in a blind for a real long time and we'd get bored, or maybe he was tired of me talking, I don't know, but anyway, he'd send me off into a thicket we'd been watching. Nothing moved for hours and then he'd send me in. He'd point out a hill in the distance, tell me to walk to the hill and back, and I'd go. I'd make sure to keep the wind at my back so the deer could smell me coming. Now, they'd move out of that thicket long before we could ever see them. But by the time I got back to my pa, those deer would be moving back into the thicket I just scared them out of. Only this time they'd usually be moving back in closer to our blind, and of course, this time we'd be ready for them.

That part I enjoyed. Walking, being in the woods, being with him.

But anyway, this time we had set up in a tree. First, we baited the clearing in front of us. Now, you fellas probably buy that deer bait from the hardware store. But my daddy swore by canned corn. It's true. You don't believe me but it's true. He'd buy a case and leave it in the cellar for a year before carrying a couple of cans out into the bush. Said it was the smell of the juice that attracted them. That's what he said. Anyway, he had poured out the two cans of corn and splashed the juice around the clearing in front of our tree stand, before he climbed up with me. We waited a long time without ever seeing anything, and we'd just started talking about me going for a walk. Heading out into the clearing we were watching and stirring up the deer. Then my pa stood up and started leaning out onto the branches of the pine tree we were in.

I was scared he was goin' to fall, and whispered to him to sit down, but he grabbed me by the collar of my coat. Whatever he was looking at, he never took his eyes off of it. He looked frantic, bug-eyed. I'd never seen my daddy scared, but that's what he was: scared. He just reached down, grabbed me, and pulled me up onto my feet. I had to hold on to the branches in front of me to keep from falling. But when I was standing I could see what he was looking at and why he was scared.

It was really far away, a hundred yards at least, but I could tell it was huge. Maybe ten or twelve feet tall, covered in long, black matted fur and moving fast. It was taking huge strides with its long legs and its long arms were swinging as it walked through the thicket. I knew as soon as I saw it. No doubt in my mind. We were looking at a sasquatch.

It's true, I swear. I told you that you weren't going to believe me but it's true. My pa and I saw a sasquatch. Anyway, after he knew that I was seeing what he was seeing, my daddy grabbed the binoculars that were hanging from my neck. He wasn't going to take his eyes off that thing for fear of losing it, so he just reached over and pulled them over my head. Clipped my nose with the strap as he pulled the loop over my head, if I remember. Then he raised them up and tried to focus. When I realized what he was doing I grabbed his .22 and did the same thing with the scope on the rifle as soon as I was able to get the focus set. See, my hands were shaking pretty bad.

When I was able to focus the scope, I was struck by how human it looked. I don't mean the having-arms-and-legs, walking-upright stuff. Sure, it was tall with broad shoulders, just like any large man. It was more than that. It was the eyes; they were blue. They were bright and keen. They were human eyes. In fact, if you ignored the fur, it was just the mouth that made it look like an animal. You know what I mean? It stuck out of its face like … like a wolf, no, more like a baboon that you see at the zoo. It had a muzzle that was full of huge fangs. Of course, I couldn't see those then, no. But I'd see those teeth later.

So I was just watching it walk. Travelin' a straight shot right across the thicket that me and my pa were watching. It took huge strides and it never once missed a step. I mean, when you watch deer, you'll see them meander and roam. A deer will stop and turn as it picks its way around trees and bushes. But not the sasquatch, no. It had a destination in mind and it knew where it was going. It walked with a purpose, not like a grazing animal, but like a person who has somewhere to be.

See, both the deer and the sasquatch had lived all their lives in the woods but the sasquatch could remember the path through the forest. It could think and remember. Just like a person.

Anyways, I was watching this thing and I realized that I was about to lose sight of it. It was only about a dozen or so feet from the edge of the forest and moving fast. In about four strides this thing was goin' to reach a cluster of trees and then I'd never be able to see it once it was in the forest. So, I was trying to think of what to do and then it stopped. It just froze. Then it turned and looked at me. A hundred yards away and it looked right at me. Not just in my direction, not toward the tree stand. It looked right at me, that's how I could see that its eyes were blue. It was looking at me. It stood still for a few seconds, then it headed into the trees. Only this time, it wasn't walking, it ran. Faster than any animal I've ever seen. Boom. A few quick strides and it vanished into the forest.

My pa must have seen the same thing 'cause by the time I lowered his .22, he was already climbing down from our tree stand. He was just a few rungs down when he shouted up for me to bring the rifle, then he jumped down the rest of the way and ran off in the direction of the creature.

I grabbed our bag and his rifle, and by the time I caught up with him, he was on a ridge a couple yards from our tree stand that overlooked the big clearing where we had seen it. He was looking through the binoculars at the spot where the creature had entered the forest. When I walked up to him I was out of breath, the excitement and the climb down wore me out in an instant. But as soon as I reached him, he started walking off in the direction of the sasquatch.

I was trying to be quiet just like he taught me, but my legs were a lot shorter than his, I was out of breath and struggling to keep up as he picked his way through the thicket to the woods. He was weaving around bushes and fallen trees. I ran up behind him and whispered, out of breath, "You saw it, too, what was that?" He said only one thing as we hustled as best we could through the tall grass. He never took his eyes off the spot where it had entered the forest, he just whispered back, "Sasquatch."

When we reached the edge of the trees, he stopped and scanned the area. He swept his head as far as he could to the left, then to the right and back again. Then he grabbed the rifle that I had slung over my shoulder. He checked it over, made sure the clip was loaded, there was a bullet in the chamber, and the safety was off. Now, my pa was always safe with his guns, so when he took the safety off I knew two things were true. One, he thought the animal was close. Very close. And two, he thought he would only get one chance. And he wanted to be ready.

So he pointed to the ground and we both crouched down and he leaned in to whisper, "See the tracks?" At first, I couldn't see nothing. I had got pretty good at tracking deer, but this was different. I was used to looking for little prints in the grass, clear footprints spaced close together. But the sasquatch see, it had huge legs and was running at top speed. So its steps had to be eight feet apart. Now, with all them leaves covering the forest floor, it would have been impossible to track a small animal, something like a rabbit, 'cause they can run without barely moving a leaf. But this thing was so big and running so fast that it left behind huge tracks in the leaves. Every eight feet there was a patch of bare ground where its steps had brushed aside all the leaves. Once I knew what we were looking for, it was going to be very easy to follow.

Pa stood up and waved me in behind him. I followed him through the forest as we walked from track to track, following the sasquatch. We were headed in almost a perfectly straight line. Again, the creature was moving with a purpose, it was headed somewhere specific.

As you know, it can get late pretty early in the woods and I was struck by how fast it was getting dark. The sun was just starting to set, but it was also getting cloudy, and in the thick forest not much light was getting through. We walked for a long time in silence. Never had no sign of the creature, but the tracks were consistent, clear, and easy to follow. With every four or five steps of ours, we'd see one of those patches where the sasquatch's step had disturbed the leaves. Never turning, just a straight line into the woods. Leading deep into the woods.

By the time we reached the clearing, it was pretty dark. I couldn't see more than a few feet before the shadows started to trick my eyes. I was sure that every tree and every bush had a monster behind it ready to tear me to shreds. But my pa, see, he was a smart hunter. He kept following the trail. Rifle butted up firm against his shoulder, finger on the guard ready to move to the trigger at the first sight of the monster. He knew that if the sasquatch kept going in a straight line, then he'd see it before it even knew it was being followed.

Eventually, Pa and I made it to a clearing. And I don't just mean a space in the trees, I mean a clearing. A big open circle of cleared ground. Maybe thirty feet where the leaves were all gone and there was nothing but a dirt-covered forest floor. Around the edge of the circle was a low thorny hedge. Looked to me like barberry bushes, about waist-high on my pa. Behind that, the trees came back huge and dense. We walked into the clearing through a gap in the bushes and then we both saw it: a green backpack leaning up against the hedge on the far side.

It was one of those old hiker packs. Dark green canvas with the aluminum tubes on the sides. Just leaning up against the hedge like some camper had just put it down to take a rest. Only it was old. The green was faded from the sun and the shoulder straps were worn and ripped. Both Pa and I were staring at the backpack as we walked into the clearing to investigate. I guess Pa was thinking there might be a person to go with that pack, 'cause he lowered the rifle.

I was starting to think that the backpack looked empty. All the flaps were hanging loose and the canvas was flat against the frame. I thought, *Why would anyone take the care to leave an old, empty backpack out like that?* Like, if you were hiking and you were going to empty your pack and leave it behind, why wouldn't you just drop it? Why prop it up in the far end of a clearing? Especially when you'd have to walk all the way back to the gap in the bushes to get back out. I was about to ask my pa if it seemed funny to him when we both noticed the mud.

We were about halfway across the circle when suddenly the dirt under our feet turned to mud. It was deep and I sank in up to my ankle with my next step. The ground was wet and heavy and clung to my boots when I took a step. There hadn't been rain in a few days but there in the centre of the clearing was a deep mud puddle. Pa stopped, still looking toward the abandoned backpack. I started to turn around, hoping to go back the way I came and circle around the puddle. But the mud stuck to me. Jammed in the treads of my boots and globbed onto the soles. It felt like I was carrying an extra five pounds on each foot, and with wet mud all over the bottoms of my boots, I could barely get any traction when I walked. Pa noticed before I had even considered it, from behind me he said, "They set a trap, run."

I was young and not really thinking, so instead of sprinting out of there I turned around like a fool and said, "What?" He didn't need to answer. I clued in just a little too late. Pa was already shouldering the .22 when I saw the first one come out from behind a tree. It was directly behind the spot where the backpack had been sitting. Perfectly camouflaged, the sasquatch was invisible until it stepped around the tree. Another step and it was at the edge of the thornbushes. I thought for a second that the ring of thornbushes would keep it back but the sasquatch never even broke stride. Two quick steps and it was at the other side of the circle of thorns, then it just lifted its leg and stepped right over the hedge. What would have been more than waist-high on me was barely above the knee for the monster. Its blue eyes flashed at me out of the darkness to tell me what I was too late to see for myself: we had been hunted.

I saw Pa was looking down the barrel at the beast and was wondering why he hadn't pulled the trigger when I saw what he already knew. There were more of them. Two of them on our left and two more on our right. Heck, there could have been a bunch more, there was no way to know. Their coarse black fur was the perfect camouflage for the dark, dense forest. But I can tell you this: there were at least four others and they were all about to take that same simple step over the hedge and then they would all be in the circle with us. We were surrounded.

I know what you are thinking, 'cause I was thinking the same thing at the time: Why didn't he shoot? Well, he did but he knew he was only going to get one shot. See, those things moved so fast that if he had shot one of them, by the time my pa pulled back the bolt on the old .22 and got a new bullet in the breach, well, we would have been goners before he took that second shot. Besides, while a .22 is enough to go rabbit- or deer-hunting, I doubt it would have been able to do much to something that big. My pa knew he had one shot and it wasn't going to do much. So he was going to save it until it could make a difference.

Pa grabbed my shoulder and threw me to the ground in the direction that we had just come. I fell on my hands and knees in the mud and that's when he pulled the trigger. He was shooting directly over me. It was a deafening crack from just a few feet away from where I was in the cold mud. I looked up to see what he was shooting at and I saw one of the creatures standing in the gap of the hedge, right where we had come in and right where we were goin' to try and leave. This one was the trailer, the last part of their plan. This sasquatch was the one that was supposed to seal off our exit once we were in their trap.

Pa had hit it square in the chest, but just like I expected, it didn't drop the big animal. But it staggered it. The sasquatch fell back against an oak tree just to the side of the path we were planning to escape through. Pa didn't bother to load another cartridge, he just threw himself down in the mud beside me and started to crawl. On all fours, we had a lot more traction than trying to stand on mud-caked boots. Digging in his elbows and keeping the rifle up to keep it out of the mud, he shouted, "Come on!" at me, and we scrambled out of the mud pit and toward the wounded animal.

Pa was back on his feet sooner than me; I was small and scared. So when he passed me he grabbed the back of my coat and pulled me up to my feet. As we ran past the wounded sasquatch, it roared and that's when I saw its teeth. It looked like a lion's mouth. Its mouth was filled with rows of long, sharp teeth but it was the fangs that gave me nightmares. Four huge fangs, two on the top and two on the bottom, longer than a man's fingers. Yellow and slick and rooted deep in black gums. When an animal's got teeth like those, they are used for only one thing: killing. They would open up on either side of a throat or the back of a neck, and cut through until they touched. Bone, tendon, spine, muscle, or even my orange hunting jacket, whatever got between those sickening teeth was going to be torn in half. I had nightmares about those yellow fangs and black gums for years.

As we ran back along the path, I looked behind to see if we were being chased but all I saw were five other monsters stopping just outside the clearing. They were checking on the wounded one. They could have chased us down easily. But they didn't. They knew their friend needed help. They were smart enough to get us to follow them, lead us into their trap, and when their plan failed and their friend was hurt, they were smart enough to let their prey go.

That's it. That's the story. I never went back in the woods again, and when I was old enough I moved here to the city.

With that, the man in charge smiles and grabs a glass from behind him saying, "See, I told you, boys, it's a hell of a good story. 'The Sasquatch Hunter' I like to call that one, and no matter how many times he tells it, it's worth every drop." Then the bartender fills the glass with beer from the tap and delivers it to the table where the old man sits alone.

The old man takes a quick sip, he is thirsty after telling the long story but he also desperately needs that drink. His hands have been shaking for hours now. He thinks briefly about pushing the glass back to the bartender, but only briefly. His second taste is long and deep; he reminds himself to take his time. Once this drink is done, the bartender will tell him to leave, then it's back outside in the cold.

The only other customers in the dingy pub finish their glasses and motion to the bartender for refills. The smiling man says with a chuckle, "And they get taller every time, too. And is it *sasquatches* or just *sasquatch*? Is it like the word *horse*, or is it like the word *moose*?" He starts laughing, delighted with how funny he thinks he is. "Or, let me guess, your pa didn't get a chance to ask them?"

His drinking buddy, who is not laughing or smiling, takes his fresh drink from the bartender and says, "What I don't get is, what's with the backpack? Why put a backpack in the clearing?"

The old man does not answer, he got what he wanted: his drink. They got what they wanted: a chance to laugh at an old man and his bizarre tale.

"Seriously," says the other patron, bringing up his question again. "Why the backpack?" When he gets no answer, he offers the old man another drink. "Tell me about the backpack and I'll buy you another beer." The old man feels he has no choice but to answer. It's not just that he wants the beer, he also wants them to understand.

"They're hunters. Hunters with keen senses, deadly weapons, and perfect camouflage," he says looking down at his now half-empty beer. "They baited us. Instead of food, they used one of their own to draw us out. Then it left a trail that was easy to follow to lead us right to their trap. A trap that was hard to get out of, and we didn't even know we were in it until it was too late. They even added a lure to make sure our attention was focused on only one thing: the backpack." With that, the old man finishes his free drink and the bartender brings him his second of the night.

The old man looks up before taking a sip and says, "The backpack always bothered me, too. But 'cause it was old. It was very old and pretty beat up. Makes me wonder how long they'd been using it as bait. They could have been using it for years, maybe decades? Using it to lure hikers away from the main trails. Using it to separate individual hunters from a group. Using it to distract campers, getting them to drop their guard just long enough to strike. Years and years of picking people off one or two at a time. Makes me think. That backpack makes me think. Think that maybe sasquatches aren't really that rare. Maybe there's lots of them. But maybe no one else ever got away from nature's greatest hunters."

ACKNOWLEDGEMENTS

THIS BOOK WOULD NOT HAVE been possible without the encouragement, hard work, and dedication of a lot of people. Like the author's family. They are a loving and encouraging bunch. But a special thanks goes to my kids and my nieces and nephews. They were quickly recruited to be my test audience and proved to be invaluable in the development of these stories. Feedback like "I like the gross part," "you should add more gross stuff," and "add even more gross stuff" was obviously taken to heart.

The hard-working team at Dundurn Press has been supportive, kind, and never short on crazy ideas. I love that. With everything they do, they are trying to make my work as good as it can be, and that is greatly appreciated.

Every great story starts with an idea; I am lucky enough to have a perfect pair of brainstorming buddies. John Titley and Drew Kozub were essential in the idea stage of this book. While that does not entitle them to any financial rewards (I have already checked with my lawyers), they will always have my gratitude and friendship.

Many of these stories were the result of invitations by teachers to join their classrooms. The first invitation came from my friend Anne Marie Butters. She is an inspiring educator who showed me that my stories can be valuable in a classroom, then worked hard to help others see it as well. Thank you, Mrs. Butters.

Most importantly, the author would not have been able to create these stories without the love, support, and understanding of his wife. She has raised three wonderful children, made several houses into homes, and handled each challenge of their long marriage with dignity and grace. Her love means the world to me.

ABOUT THE AUTHOR

JEREMY JOHN IS CURRENTLY ranked as the sixty-second most famous person from Brantford, Ontario. (Look it up. There are a lot.) Jeremy had a career in radio and television, including several years on *Breakfast Television* in Winnipeg, a one-of-a-kind place filled with people he quickly grew to love. He also had what may be the world record for shortest professional baseball career, playing a single game with the Winnipeg Goldeyes before retiring due to being old, uncoordinated, and out-of-shape. Lately, he has been spending time pretending to be a woodworker, cheering for and complaining about his beloved Toronto Blue Jays, and arguing about politics with anyone unfortunate enough to listen. Jeremy now lives with his wife and kids, plus a dog he pretends not to like, in Sudbury, Ontario.

UNLOCK AN EXTRA SPOOKY STORY
BY COMPLETING THE HAUNTED
BOOKSTORE ESCAPE ROOM!

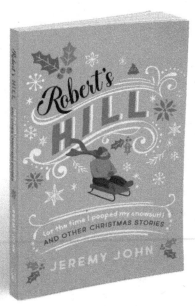